Please return item by last date shown, or contact library to renew

LP 3

DEAD LETTERS

Before committing suicide, Harold Grant posts three letters — one to his wife, one to his business partner, and one to a third party. The first two letters are highly damaging to their recipients, who dare not show them to the police. But who has got the third letter, and what does it say? The recipients of the first two are sick with anxiety on this score. Thus begins a strange chain of events, out of which develop both a love affair and a bloody murder . . .

JOHN BURKE

DEAD LETTERS

Complete and Unabridged

LINFORD
Leicester

First published in Great Britain

First Linford Edition
published 2014

A catalogue record for this book is available
from the British Library.

ISBN 978–1–4448–2012–6

Published by
F. A. Thorpe (Publishing)
Anstey, Leicestershire

Set by Words & Graphics Ltd.
Anstey, Leicestershire
Printed and bound in Great Britain by
T. J. International Ltd., Padstow, Cornwall

This book is printed on acid-free paper

For Peter who started it on its way

1

Writing the letters was the last pleasure he would have on this earth. He savoured it to the full. It was long enough since he'd had anything that could reasonably be called pleasure.

First the one to his wife.

Then one for his brother-in-law. This was more detailed, spelling out the whole story. Not that it needed spelling out to Norman of all people; but he had always been meticulous and now instinctively needed to justify himself, to tidy up and trim the ends neatly. Writing it all out in full was both an indictment and a last cleansing confession before he put an end to the whole grubby business.

When he had signed the second letter he sat back. He wouldn't have minded a drink, but all the drink was downstairs. Even in his most despairing moments he had never got round to keeping a bottle up here in his study. To go down now would be to face inevitable questions.

There was a faint mutter through the drainpipe, which made a diagonal beneath his window, and the rush of water into the drain. That meant Arlene was back, in the shower after her round of golf.

He stayed where he was and addressed the two envelopes.

Once he had posted them, there would be no turning back. The thought didn't frighten him. He didn't want to turn back.

* * *

Today had been only marginally worse than most recent days, but just bad enough to tip the scales.

Norman had asked him to handle a job that would normally have been allocated to one of the regular chasers.

But everyone was tied up — three of them on a big company check-up that promised big dividends.

'Do you good to get out and about a bit,' Norman had said boisterously. 'See what it's like in the field.'

So he had got out. He had played it

Norman's way. And once he tackled a job, however distasteful, he had to do it just as efficiently as it could humanly be done. Norman knew this, laughed at it, and had played on it for years

The man he had to see lived on the outskirts of St. Albans in a house with a neglected front garden and window frames sorely in need of a coat of paint. His name was Westwood. One Saturday afternoon be had been into the town and bought two beds, a sideboard, a dining room suite and an armchair on hire purchase. That same afternoon he had gone on to the electrical department of another store and bought a standard lamp and a television set, also on hire purchase. The following week the two cheques he had signed for the deposits bounced. After an exchange of arguments and an intensification of threats from the two stores, he had paid less than half the deposit money and promised to make it up within the month; but was defaulting on his payments.

It was an old stunt. In the normal run of things a status man would hurry round before delivery was made to assess the credit rating of a customer wanting to take on a heavy hire purchase commitment. But on a Saturday, store managers were glad to make quick sales, spurred on by aggressive telephone calls from head office late on Friday asking why turnover was sagging and what they were doing to get stock on the move. A large sale on Saturday would show up healthily in the books for that week. With the customer wanting to take the stuff away as fast as possible, there was no time for a debt check-up: the security officer on the premises, usually an ex-policeman, would take a quick, surreptitious look at the customer and make a snap judgment. Unless the customer was a known trickster or visibly a shifty type, he would almost certainly be accepted.

Westwood was not visibly a shifty type. When he opened the door he was wearing a candy-striped shirt and blue slacks which were shabby but had once been good; he had a supercilious mouth and coldly candid eyes; his voice had just the right arrogance to impress a salesman or floor manager.

4

'Yes?'

'Mr. Westwood — Mr. Robert Westwood?'

'That's right.' His eyes stared over the garden and the tangled hedge, and with a touch of peevishness he said: 'Is that van yours?'

'It is.'

'Do you have to park it right outside my house?'

It often affected them like that. However derisive they might be of honest dealing and the stuffiness of their conventional neighbours, they got twitchy when a van rolled up at their door bearing in large red letters the name of PLEDGE AND DISTRAINT SERVICES.

'May I come in?'

This could be a tricky moment. This was when you could get doors slammed in your face, or a spattering of curses.

Westwood stood aside.

Which meant he was as good as defeated. Once they let you in, you stayed in and wore them down.

Westwood was pathetically less impressive in his own sitting room than he had presumably been in the shop. The arrogance faded into petulance. He said:

'I don't know why you have to come round pestering like this.'

He was young — and already a failure. His wife and two small children were sprawled in front of the television set watching some film about a princess and an enchanted watermill. The woman, with a fine bony face and lank black hair, glanced up incuriously and then concentrated once more on the screen. But she sighed, as though knowing what was going to happen. Even Westwood's eyes flickered towards the set compulsively.

'You are Mr. Robert Westwood, and you have a hire purchase commitment which you have allowed to lapse on several items of furniture, namely — '

'All right, you don't need to recite the list.'

'Are you prepared to settle now for the back payments due, and to maintain regular payments from now on?'

'I would if I could.' Westwood spoke as though it didn't matter a damn: he was only making conversation while he watched the film. 'It just so happens I'm out of work at the moment.'

'When do you expect to find another job?'

Westwood shrugged. 'Haven't the foggiest.'

'Were you in work when you ordered all this furniture?'

'Don't remember. Probably not.'

'You do realise that that's not just irresponsible, but criminal?' It sounded pompous, but he was angry. Shiftlessness of this kind always made him angry. At the same time he was angry with himself for being here at all.

The two children looked round, sullen with antagonism because he was interrupting their programme.

Westwood said: 'Well, what are you going to do about it?'

'We could take you to Court.'

Silently he prayed it wouldn't come to that. The judge would condemn the firm for not being more cautious, would lecture the defaulter, and would then suspend any sentence for three months, to give the man a chance to find work and redeem himself. If Westwood malingered and came up in Court again, there would be further costs to the firm, he would probably prove to have plenty of other outstanding debts, and in the end the best order you could hope for would be in the region of twenty pence a week.

Fortunately Westwood wasn't quite as fly as that. He said: 'Well, that's up to you, isn't it? Or . . . ?'

'Or I can take the furniture away.'

'All right. Take it.'

His wife forced herself to get up and turn her back on the television set. 'You've got to leave us a bed. And one for the kids.'

'I'm afraid it's not up to me to select items which can remain.'

He went to the front door and waved. The two men from the van headed for the gate and the crazy-paving path.

'Look,' said Westwood, 'give us time to pack it all up properly. Come back tomorrow, and it'll all be ready.'

Come back tomorrow, and the house would be empty. Somehow they would have got away somewhere with their belongings and all the things that didn't belong to them.

'I think we'll take them now.'

'Leave us a bed,' the woman said again.

The two men came in and set to work. The children began to howl as the television was disconnected. Westwood dejectedly watched the picture shrink to a pinpoint.

'You may as well leave the mattress,' he said. 'The kids have weed on it God knows how many times already. You wouldn't want it for anyone else.'

When the last chair had been carried out to the van, the woman said: 'You might at least have let them see the end of their serial.'

'Don't you worry,' said Westwood with vague tenderness. 'We'll get another set.'

'It's my duty to warn you,' — the anger had gone, it left him sick and empty, with hardly the strength to parrot through the routine — 'that reclamation of the goods does not necessarily mean that you will not in due course be prosecuted.'

Westwood looked round the bare room and shrugged with some of his old contemptuous manner. Come and prosecute, he sourly invited.

The van moved off.

'You didn't take long over that one,' said the driver.

'It was pretty straightforward.'

'That doesn't mean they always give in so easily.' The driver touched a faint blue mark along his left temple. 'Got that six months ago. Still shows, doesn't it? Bloke with an iron bar.'

'Our Mr. Westwood wasn't that sort.'

'Layabouts,' said the driver with sudden vehemence. 'Got no time for them.'

He agreed with the driver. He knew all the arguments: many of them were his own arguments. People oughtn't to get into debt in the first place. They oughtn't to put others in the position of having to waste time and money chasing them. All the postage, the telephone calls, the legal procedures . . . He had no sympathy for such folk, despised everything they stood for — if you could call it standing — yet now despised what he had just had to do.

He saw the clock face of a memorial tower on the roundabout ahead, and said: 'I won't come all the way back with you. Drop me by the bus stop.'

The bus took nearly an hour, but he was glad of the lull. As it joggled past shop fronts, then up a long suburban hill through a leafy lane and on past more, smaller shop fronts, he found that he had made up his mind.

The decision once made, he was quite calm. The tensions and miseries sloughed away. There was no need to add up pros and cons and strike a balance. It must all have been working itself out at the back of his mind for some considerable time now: the solution, when it came, was sharp and clear and irrefutable.

He got off the bus by the olde-worlde inn dating from 1931, and walked up the slope.

At the top was a house, his own house — only of course it was nominally not his any more — which he looked at as though for the first time . . . only of course it was the last time. Set within a palisade of spruce and fir, dark against the beeches gleaming along the canal and masking the railway line, it was half-timbered and had twisting neo-Elizabethan chimneys, and a long brick wall with a filigree wrought-iron gateway

11

opening on to the rose garden; and he thought he had never seen anything so ridiculous.

He went in.

Amanda sprawled on the white rug listening to her transistor. A pop group including an electronic organ was playing a chart-topping version of the St. Anthony Chorale. She snipped with long scissors at greasy yellow fur round the neck of an ancient coat for which she had probably paid more in a boutique than she would have paid for a new dress in Bond Street.

He looked a vague question, and she said: 'Mummy's out. Playing a round at the Club.' She laughed. 'I mean,' she enunciated with sniggering precision, 'playing a round. Not playing around.'

The joke wasn't relevant to anything or anybody. Her mother didn't play around, at the Club or elsewhere else. Her mother craved the prestige, not the passion.

He went upstairs and wrote the obligatory letters. The sentences arrived trim and ready-to-wear. It was as though someone wiser than himself had decreed that for his own good he must be seen swiftly through the final stages.

How many tens of thousands of times had he signed his name in that chunky black handwriting? Never again.

As water gurgled into the drain below his window he had a sharp picture of Arlene in the shower: Arlene with her head back, the water cascading down her throat and gleaming over her shoulders.

He sat quite still for a full minute. He mustn't weaken now.

Then he got up and went along the landing, telling himself he was going to the loo.

Their bedroom door was open. As he looked in, Arlene crossed the room, naked, from the door leading to their bathroom.

It had happened before. Was he going to let it happen again: going to let her pull him back from the brink? They had quarrelled so many times — or, even worse, had gone their separate ways under this same roof with hardly a word to say to each other for weeks on end — and then he had been shaken again into awareness of the beauty of that tall, sleek, strong body. He had tried to believe she was worth it after all and that they could still make sense out of being married; must have made a hundred attempts to believe. But in spite of her Amazonian perfection, the swaggering haunches and the breasts she used to stroke musingly in front of her mirror, Arlene was cold.

Still he couldn't move away from the door. He had hoped so often. He was still tempted.

Arlene said: 'What on earth have you been doing, shut away in there?'

He moved a step towards her. There was the scent of her, straight from the hot water and the soap and the cold water. Her skin gleamed, still faintly damp. Her lips glistened.

He said: 'I've been . . . writing a couple of letters.'

'Why couldn't you have done them before you left the office?'

She saw his eyes measuring her and half turned away, not coyly but resentfully.

'I was out on a job,' he explained, as though it mattered. 'I came straight home.'

'I didn't see the car when I got back.'

'It's still in the office park.'

'A bit stupid.'

'It won't come to any harm.'

'How are you going to get there in the morning?'

He ought perhaps to tell her straight, here and now, that for him there wasn't going to be a morning. But the complications, the inevitable row . . . No, he wanted his last moments to be quiet and undisturbed.

'Knocking off early,' she was saying. She reached for her tawny spotted dressing gown. 'And why couldn't your letters wait till tomorrow, anyway?'

'I wanted them done now.'

'You're not telling me you've got something so important to write that it couldn't wait another day?'

He was wasting his time. He turned back towards his study. But she didn't like that. She didn't want him, but she didn't want him to be out of range. She followed

15

him, making it up as she went along: 'Really, if you're going to start working overtime . . . I mean, knocking off early in order to bring work home . . . ' She plucked at his attention, laughing the crackly laugh he had once thought was sensual and alluring.

He went into his room and closed the door, half afraid she might keep coming. But that would have made it seem important, which she didn't want anything connected with her husband to seem.

It took his breath away, realizing how much he disliked her. And Amanda. And Nigel, going off to school with a limp handshake and a grin of indifference.

He sat and stared at the two envelopes. It would have been more sensible to have gone straight out to the pillar box with them instead of letting himself be distracted.

A cupboard door slammed. A drawer screeched open and shut. Arlene was making as much noise as possible.

He would give her time to dress and go downstairs.

If it hadn't been for that need to fill in a few minutes, he might never have written the third letter.

⋆   ⋆   ⋆

To hide the bulge of the gun in his inside pocket he slipped his overcoat on as soon as he reached the hall. He longed to leave the house without any further talk. But there was a stupid reason why he couldn't.

He hadn't got any postage stamps.

Two of the letters could, of course, be propped up on Arlene's dressing table. One for her and one to be passed on to Norman. But not the third: they'd be unable to resist opening it, and its chances of being passed on then would be small. Safer, and somehow a right and proper part of the ritual, that they should be individually delivered after he was gone.

Through the sitting room doorway he saw Arlene flipping over pages of a magazine. She had been waiting for him to come down.

He went in and said: 'Anybody got any stamps?'

17

'You're not rushing out now, are you?'

'I'll just go to the box down the road.'

'Amanda can go for you.'

'Aw,' said Amanda.

He thought of her reading the addresses and coming back and asking whatever he was up to, and Arlene chiming in and asking, and asking . . .

'I've got my coat on now,' he said. 'All I want is some stamps.'

'First class or second class?' asked Amanda, prepared to be obliging provided she didn't have to get up and run the errand for him.

'First class, I'm sure,' said her mother. 'These letters must be top priority.'

'First class,' he said.

'How many?' Amanda rolled over on the rug, groped for a shoulder bag she had tossed on to a chair, and dipped into it.

'Three, please.'

When she had passed them to him her hand remained outstretched. He dropped the coins into her palm, and she dropped them loose into her bag.

'Why can't they go with the office mail in the morning?' Arlene couldn't bear to

18

stop worrying at it. 'What's so very special . . . ?'

He escaped. The evening was cold but still. A faint piney smell came from a heap of logs in the pub yard, waiting to be loaded into the lounge fireplace with its surround of horse brasses and warming-pans. He was fleetingly reminded of the tang on the air in that Welsh village where he had spent so many holidays with his aunt. Things then had seemed so good. The promise of those days had proved a ridiculous fraud.

Somebody inside the pub laughed. He debated whether to go in and have a last pint. It would give them something to talk about afterwards. Came in and had a drink, you'd never have known . . . oh, I wouldn't say that, I *thought* there was something wrong . . . must have been only a few minutes before he did it.

He crossed the road to the red shaft of the pillar box on the opposite corner. The plop of his suicide letters in the box was like a guillotine blade falling on his neck.

Too late to go back now.

The words had a lovely reassuring ring.

Too late: He wanted it to be too late.

The mud in the lane had hardened. He limped towards the canal towpath, absurdly anxious not to trip in a rut and sprain an ankle.

A tenuous breath of mist hung above the canal. He settled himself at the water's edge and took out the revolver. He had had it since the brutal days in Korea. It was warm from his pocket and, like the words too late, snug and comforting . . .

Even in Korea there had been hope. They had fought, and saw hope in the distance, beyond the end of fighting; cursed and killed, and snarled among themselves, and still promised themselves a bash at all the things waiting to be done when this was over.

So many things he ought to have done.

If he sat at a certain angle as he fired, his body would topple into the water. They might not find him for several days. That would complicate things for them. He allowed himself a moment of self-indulgent malice at the thought of Norman and Arlene opening their envelopes. All the trouble and notoriety. He was only sorry he couldn't be around to see it.

He was committing suicide out of contempt rather than despair; out of a great, sick boredom.

Somewhere a fallen twig cracked. Footsteps scuffed along the lane.

Let them pass.

But why? Someone would sooner or later have to find him. No reason why it shouldn't be now. No reason why the doorbell shouldn't drag Arlene away from the magazine she was pretending to read.

The footsteps came closer. He lifted the revolver.

2

The letters were stacked as neatly as always on the blotter. At the top were the trivial items. The sequence built up, or rather down, to the livelier stuff at the bottom. His secretary had sensed, before Norman Leggett had put it into words or even acknowledged it to himself, his need for drama even in the everyday routine. She was an exceptional secretary. They played a game of mutual needling: he would try to catch her out, accusing her of getting the priorities wrong this morning or that — and she would laugh, and parry, and defend her choice, and be right nine times out of ten. After five years she still called him Mr. Leggett and he called her Mrs. Barsham.

On this Friday morning he skimmed the letters, put aside one with a cheque stapled to it, and thumbed the buzzer.

Mrs. Barsham was wearing her turquoise-rimmed glasses, and some time the previous day had managed to have a rinse that gleamed silver from one angle, mauve from another. She sat down, crossed her legs, flipped open her shorthand pad, and laid her pencil across it from corner to corner. She said:

'Good morning, Mr. Leggett.'

'Good morning, Mrs. Barsham.'

One pencil-thin eyebrow arched a query. Was there going to be a challenge this morning?

Norman said: 'Let's have a quick run through the Green Ink accounts.'

Unhesitatingly, she pulled his nearer filing tray three inches towards her edge of the desk, removed the top sheet, and handed it to him.

Mrs. Barsham was thirty. She had married an English importer and exporter of skins and hides while he was on a business trip to Cologne, had come to England with him, and four years later had divorced him. For the last of those four years and for the next four she had worked for Norman. Her German accent had been reduced to the ghost of a lisp, no more than the intimation of an attractively alien music in the pitch of the syllables. She was tautly loyal to Norman: she protected him from troublesome outsiders, hated those who found ways of getting past her, and despised those who weren't wily enough to get past her. Some favoured clients on especially friendly terms with Norman would nudge him, chuckle, and hint that he'd got it made, hadn't he?

They were wrong. Decorative status symbol as she was, Mrs. Barsham made no emotional demands. They were allies in business, just as he and his sister were. It was better that way. Getting too involved, he would have destroyed a stimulating, beautifully balanced relationship.

He checked the incoming mail against the list. 'I think our friends in Neasden had better go on the Red Ink accounts.'

'I've been afraid it would come to that.'

'Afraid? It ups our percentage after next week. If we get 'em.'

Her glasses sparked against the light. He knew how her eyes behind the glasses were contracting, widening, glinting. 'You will get them,' she said placidly. She never said 'we': responsibility and achievement were always Norman's alone.

'You saw this?' He held up the letter with the cheque attached.

'Yes, I noticed it as I went through.'

'Never thought they'd pay up.'

She toyed with her pencil, eyes demurely downcast. She had never, said the tilt of her head, had any doubts.

They tacitly shared their pleasure in the way problems worked out — or were forced to work out. Even the tiniest triumphs were exalting, even those which cost more in time and manpower than, strictly speaking, they were worth.

He went through the mail in the order she had established, dictating replies and instructions to members of the team — the light mob and the heavy mob.

When he paused, Mrs. Barsham said: 'I've got a note to remind you today's the deadline for the Tuchmann payment.'

'The Hammersmith property deal?'

'That's the one.'

'His cheque's not in?'

'No. I've checked.'

Norman reached for the phone. An eager Woolwich whine jangled in the earpiece, like the yelp of a dog fidgeting to be let loose.

'Michael, Tuchmann still hasn't paid up.'

'Shame on him.' There was a splinter of slavering laughter in the reproachful tone; the baying of one who knew he was going to be unleashed.

'Time to switch from the firm,' said Norman, 'to the bod himself. Lives in one of those luxury blocks in Holland Park. The address is on file.' He noticed that Mrs. Barsham was already writing it out from memory on a jotter, ready to send it downstairs. 'Get Charlie to ring him at eleven tonight. If he's not there, keep trying. And if he is there, keep it up anyway: every hour on the hour, over the weekend. When he's left for the office Monday morning, see he gets an envelope tucked into his letterbox. Tucked in halfway, I mean.'

'Showing 'Debt Demand' bright and clear on the outside.'

'Right. Three or four of his high-class

neighbours should spot it before the day's out.'

'And if he still won't play?'

'A personal call. Next Wednesday or Thursday, say.'

'Personal call,' breathed Michael. 'With one of the dogs?'

'Mind how you go. No harassment. Remember Section 40 of the Act.'

Michael guffawed. Norman kept a straight face. Mrs. Barsham bowed her head over her pad. The routine tagline, always uttered with religious solemnity, was always good for a laugh.

Three more letters were speedily dealt with, then Norman shot abruptly at Mrs. Barsham: 'Anything on that taxi-driver?'

She dialled an internal extension number and pursed her lips as though she could have predicted the answer without going through this procedure.

'Scarpered?' said Norman.

'He must have gone last night.'

'With all the furniture?'

She didn't bother to answer. The twitch of her shoulders was expressive enough.

'I'll tell you one thing,' vowed Norman:

'when we do find him, I'll make it bloody difficult for him to get a licence to carry on his taxi service.'

They worked their way through several other items. Some, such as three cases of refusal to pay the full interest and vacation fee on a redeemed second mortgage, were worth only a minute and a half each. Then they came to the more complex ones.

Norman rang for coffee to be sent in, and said: 'I wonder how Harold got on yesterday?' He prodded the extension switch. In spite of all that had happened to poor old Harold, he still made a point of speaking to him direct rather than leaving Mrs. Barsham to play the intermediary. They owed Harold at least that much.

There was no reply.

Mrs. Barsham said: 'He wasn't in when I came past.'

'Maybe he found yesterday's task a bit exhausting. Sleeping it off, eh?'

She allowed no flicker of disrespect in her answering smile, but they understood each other and he knew she was laughing approval inwardly.

'Funny,' Norman went on. 'I thought I saw his car in the park earlier on.'

'In exactly the same place as it was yesterday afternoon.'

He hesitated, wondering whether to ring Harold at home. Before he could make up his mind, the phone rang and Mrs. Barsham answered it. She held out the receiver towards him. 'Mrs. Grant.'

Arlene's voice asked: 'Is Harold anywhere in the building?'

'We were just saying we supposed he was still in bed.'

'He hasn't been back all night.'

'All night?' Across the phone, Norman said: 'Mrs. Barsham, ring down and ask if he got into any difficulties over that job out at — '

'No,' Arlene was saying, 'no, it's not that. He came home all right, from the job.'

'I thought you said he didn't come home.'

'He came home all right from the job,' she repeated. 'Then he shut himself in his room and wrote some letters, and insisted on going out to the post with them.'

'Letters? Who'd he be writing letters to?'

'I've no idea. I asked what was so urgent about them, and he wouldn't say.'

'Applying for another job?'

Arlene laughed metallically. 'But where is he?'

When in doubt, Norman was invariably loud and breezy. Even when he knew there'd be bad news to break within a few minutes, he prefaced it with a slap on the back. Now he said: 'Maybe he's been using some initiative, chasing up a job he's selected for himself — he'll have left a message somewhere. I'll check.'

'He was most peculiar, the way he — '

'I'll check,' said Norman, 'and ring you back.'

The two men who had been out with Harold the day before confirmed that he had asked to be dropped at a bus stop rather than come back in with them to Wembley. They had assumed he'd be going home. No, there'd been no snags over the Westwood job: in fact, he'd had the whole thing wrapped up in double quick time, without any fuss.

'A bit quiet on the way back,' remembered the driver. 'A bit thoughtful, you know. But then he often is, is Mr. Grant.'

Instead of phoning, Norman drove out to see Arlene. By the time he got there she had worked herself up into a rage.

'What the hell does he think he's playing at? Walking out like that, walking out without a word, with that silly smug look on his face . . . just flitting off . . . '

'Did he pack a bag or anything?'

'He was empty-handed when he went out. Except for the letters.'

'He couldn't have . . . ' He had no idea quite what he was groping for, quite how to put it.

'Couldn't have what?'

'Packed a bag earlier — had it hidden somewhere? Ready to clear out?'

They went up to the bedroom. Arlene wrenched open the wardrobe doors and made a quick assessment, irritably twitching suits and shirts to and fro along the rails.

'Nothing gone,' she established. 'Nothing but what he stood up in.'

In the sitting room she poured two large gins.

'Well, now,' boomed Norman, not wanting things to get too serious until he was sure just how serious they were, 'what d'you suppose he's up to? Any hint of some dolly bird tucked away somewhere? May ring tonight with some excuse, and come home the worse for wear in the morning.'

She said: 'He's been very odd lately. Brooding.'

'I thought he was coping pretty well.'

'He wouldn't talk about the way we'd organised the set-up, but it kept eating away at him.'

'Oh, now, he did fall in with everything we suggested.' We didn't give him much choice, said a scratchy voice somewhere within Norman's head; he could always out-talk that kind of voice. 'You're not going to tell me that now the worst is over he's had a brainstorm and marched out? I mean, what sort of job could he get — what's the point?'

Arlene said: 'If only we knew who those letters went to . . . '

Norman Leggett had been an account executive in an advertising agency when he met Harold Grant. He already foresaw a brighter future in public relations than in run-of-the-mill publicity. He was large, boisterous, unquenchable, never took no for an answer, and knew all the openings. Plugs that he planted in newspapers and magazines worked ten times more effectively than paid advertising. When an editor refused to play along, Norman knew a sub here or a compositor there who would cut paragraphs of authorised copy and slip in the references he wanted. They always seemed to slide through without awkward repercussions. There were reporters whose ears he could bend, gossip columnists with thirsts less expensive than the cost of artwork and plate-making. He was expert at awakening interest in a product or a person and keeping it alive by such methods as writing a condemnatory letter to a paper, attacking these opinions in a letter under another name, and answering the attack with enlightened facts and crystal-clear reasoning.

Harold Grant had been invalided out of Korea with a splintered leg, leaving him after a few years with some recurrent pain but only a slight limp. He was also left with a sceptical view of so-called military discipline. Military service had been a revelation to him — a revelation of dodging and scrounging, of corruption and bumbling inefficiency. His own war became a one-man war against waste and incompetence. He proved to be one of those officers with a flair for laying hands on things when they were needed and shifting them to where they were needed. He freed supplies which were doing nobody any good in base stores; blocked several outlets which poured straight into the black market; dug out small luxuries which in those fighting conditions were necessities rather than luxuries; was a great progress-chaser. The Americans with whom he worked showed him both antagonism and respect. He was horrified to find that prestige battles among the allies were usually of more importance than the defeat of the enemy.

Civilian life proved depressingly the same. A firm's slip-shod way of running its business echoed the blunders of whole regiments. Its internal dissensions were more bitter and destructive than all its conflicts with competitors.

Norman agreed with Harold that industry was in a mess. It needed massive reorganisation, whole new programmes for factories, offices, middlemen, the entire crowd. Between them he and Harold could sort it out.

Together they set up the firm of Interflow Consultants, and in 1953 Harold married Norman's sister Arlene.

They covered the whole spectrum of job analysis and evaluation studies, long-range planning procedures and training. They carried out appraisals of company strategy, information and communications systems, time and motion studies, and executive selection. The fortunes of Interflow itself flourished along with those of its clients. Harold impressed top executives and staff alike with his own genuine urge to reshape companies into tidier, less sprawling entities — to cut out waste, reduce paperwork, increase production.

Norman concentrated on building up the public relations side, taking on some profitable accounts and lecturing to training courses arranged by Harold for PROs from various organisations.

After ten years when it seemed they couldn't put a foot wrong, a gradual falling off of business was perceptible. The competition was fiercer. The gimmicks were gaudier. Firms tended to favour those consultants who recommended intensification rather than abolition of paperwork. Newly designed cards, forms and ledgers looked more impressive, seemed to give more value for money, than Harold Grant's spartan organigrams and austere flow charts. Complexity was a better buy than simplicity. The professional jargon became more obfuscating: like lawyers and town planners, the management consultants were building up their own mystique and their own impressive, arcane incantations.

Harold doggedly pursued the perfection of simplicity. Norman began to look warily around for profitable side issues that might be exploited. In his old agency days he had been good at spotting and annexing some nice little subsidiary lines for himself. There was that film starlet who had privately paid him a fee to get her name into the maximum possible number of periodicals, in any context whatsoever. Norman had employed his native wit, his firm's facilities, and a very small proportion of the money she had given him, and achieved more mentions of her in one week than stars earning a hundred times her salary. There was always a profit somewhere; always a better way of doing things, always *some* way of making *somebody* listen.

Diversification became one of Norman's favourite concepts.

When you were granted free access to the books and processes of a chemical works, to research laboratories or an automobile accessories plant, you were offered at the same time a golden opportunity for industrial espionage. Quiet tip-offs given to competitors by roundabout methods could pay handsomely. Risky, of course. You had to play each episode by ear.

And then Norman saw the big breakthrough.

Whenever Harold had to tidy up a staff system that had proliferated without pruning over the years rather than being planned all in one piece from the start, he inevitably had to analyse the entire accounting system, employment of capital, investments, salaries and expenditures. And inevitably on the books there would be some revelation of unnecessary delay in collecting outstanding debts, of bad debts despairingly written off, of confusion over the firm's assets and liabilities. While Harold drafted his flow diagrams and his watertight methods for control of raw material ordering, authorisations for signing cheques, handling of postage stamps and petty cash, Norman extracted details which could be assembled into dossiers specifically related to financial overstretching — and the need for efficient debt collection.

A separate company was duly set up with Norman and Arlene as directors. Pledge and Distraint Services announced themselves, in small sans serif type below their letter heading, as 'The Discreet

Debt Collectors'. Their discretion allowed the use of dogs, persistent telephone badgering, the addressing of demands 'by mistake' to next-door neighbours, a well-rehearsed litany of legal threats, and loud shouting matches on doorsteps.

It paid off. It paid lavishly.

Harold had complained: 'This isn't what we went into business for.'

'It's the key to the whole pattern.' Norman was expansive, confident. 'No firm can survive in a competitive world on extended credit. How do you expand, reinvest, install new equipment, pay reasonable dividends? Cut down the labour on follow-ups — get your money in . . . and use it.'

'I don't like these bully-boy tactics.'

'You don't like cheats either, do you? You pay your own bills on the nail — I know that. Arlene's told me so, she thinks you overdo it a bit — so why should you let other folk get away with it? Scroungers who waste time and money. Make 'em pay up.'

He overrode all Harold's objections. The debt collection operation made more

and more inroads into Interflow Consultants. The two firms shared the same
building and, to begin with, the same
staff. Gradually the more go-ahead employees were taken over by the collection agency.
There was more work there and more
money. The agency charged a sliding
scale, not merely according to the amount
recovered but with a factor for the length
of time the debt had been outstanding.
The big killings were on big company
debts, but Norman didn't scorn the little
individual jobs as well: you had to give a
comprehensive service. Within its first
eighteen months, Pledge and Distraint
Services broke even. Five years later its
annual profit after tax had risen to
£120,000. It continued to rise.

At the same time Interflow Consultants
was tottering towards bankruptcy.

Norman did nothing to stop this.
Rather, he pointed out advantages that
ought to have been clear to Harold with
his analytical mind. Any good accountant
could show how to put the situation to
good use. Their own accountant was only
too eager to do so.

Harold was persuaded to transfer his personal assets, including his holding in Pledge and Distraint Services and other investments, to his wife. She personally took out a large life insurance policy on him, while he cashed in on his own policy and handed the money over to her. Interflow Consultants was then allowed to run down gently over a nicely calculated period, until Harold filed a declaration of insolvency.

When a payout of twenty-five pence in the pound had been agreed with sundry creditors, Pledge and Distraint Services made an offer to take over what was left of the firm — useful as a tax loss — and to employ Harold at a reasonable salary.

His bankruptcy could have been discharged within a matter of weeks if it had not been for one creditor, who had supplied all their office stationery and who now refused to accept the composition of the outstanding debt.

'Let it ride,' said Norman comfortably. 'If he doesn't institute proceedings within three months, he's bound by the terms the others have agreed. I don't think he'll start anything. And if he does, I'll get him. The only reason he's being sticky is that he's got some sizeable debts of his own. I'll get his creditors as clients, and sock him on their behalf — and ours.'

Harold's house might have been claimed by the official receiver, so this was sold in good time to Norman. Harold did not ask for all the cash at once, since an outright payment could also have attracted the receiver's scythe. Instead, Norman paid Harold only the interest on what was in effect the loan of the house, and allowed Harold and his family to go on living there. The receiver could have asked for a levy on this interest, but it was understood he would not do so: the bankrupt Harold Grant had to be allowed some means of survival and regeneration.

In the event of Harold's death, his executors could give six months' notice of call-in on the full sum.

On the Saturday morning Norman had two phone calls at home, one close on the heels of the other.

Arlene was first. 'Those letters of

Harold's — I've had one of them.'

'Second-class post?'

'No, I remember he asked Amanda for . . . but, Norman, what he's done . . . '

'Bloody post goes from bad to worse. Two flaming days to get from the box at the corner of your lane to your front door. Or did he post it somewhere else?' He heard the harsh, unsteady rustle of her breath at the other end. 'Look, where is he? What *has* he done?'

'He's dead. Norman, he's killed himself.'

The stupid nit. Of all the stupid, feeble, pathetic things to do.

Aloud he said: 'You're sure?'

'It's all in the letter. That's why he went out on Thursday night. Writing this, and then . . . '

'Look, just what does he say?'

'I'm not going to read it over the phone. I'm just not.' Her voice was higher than usual. It trembled with what might have been real horror, or fury.

'I'll come right over,' said Norman.

Stupid nit. Poor, wet old Harold.

Not our fault. Nothing to do with us. I

43

was always fond of him. He knew that. A bit of a mug, but we got along fine. To go and cave in like that . . . He was about to set out when the phone rang again.

Mrs. Barsham went meticulously to the office every Saturday morning in case anything in the mail needed his personal attention. She would report over the phone, so that he could contact duty men and get them moving if the occasion demanded. In urgent cases he would drive over to Wembley himself.

Mrs. Barsham said: 'There's a letter marked 'Personal and Confidential'.'

There often were. You got them all the time: people hoping the world wasn't going to be let in on their shifty little secrets.

'Open it,' he said. 'If it's anything important, read it out to me.'

'It's in Mr. Grant's handwriting.'

She was waiting for him to say that it was all right, that she should still open it and read it out. He trusted her. The firm had no secrets from her.

He heard a far echo of Arlene's shaky voice. He said: 'Can you bring it out here?

I'm afraid we've had rather bad news.'

'About Mr. Grant?'

'He's dead. Please bring the letter.'

He phoned Arlene back and asked if she would drive over here instead of his going to her place. When he told her there was another letter on its way, she was silent for so long he thought the line had gone dead. Then: 'I'll start now.'

Poor old Harold. He had liked Harold, of course he had liked him. Norman always liked to like people, even when necessity forced him to harry them. And he liked to be liked.

Arlene and Mrs. Barsham arrived almost simultaneously. Arlene watched mute, as he tore open the envelope. She clutched her own letter, folded, in her right hand. Mrs. Barsham moved a few discreet steps away and began automatically to tidy Norman's cluttered writing table.

'It can't be true, can it?' The words were torn from Arlene as he began to read his letter. 'He can't have done it.'

'Looks as though he has.' Norman shook his head. 'Poor old Harold. I don't get it.' Then, as he turned the page and

45

read on with shuddering incredulity: 'The bastard. The miserable, creepy little bastard.'

When he had finished he reached numbly for the one Arlene was holding. It was different, more personal, less detailed; but just as deadly in its own uncompromising way.

Mrs. Barsham cleared her throat and said: 'I'll go back to the office, Mr. Leggett. If you want anything — '

'You can go home,' he said abstractedly.

'I'd prefer to stay in the office. Just in case there's anything at all I can do.'

He didn't argue. He wasn't interested. Mrs. Barsham shook hands with Arlene and said with just the right solemnity: 'I am so very sorry, Mrs. Grant. This is a terrible event. So sad.'

When she had gone, Norman compulsively read the two letters right through again. One thing was certain: they weren't the kind of suicide letter you'd dare to show the police or the coroner.

Which made things difficult. Because . . .

He looked, stunned, at Arlene. She was very white, with two gashes of shadow straining across the corners of her mouth. They had always been close. As children they hadn't needed to finish sentences when they were together, but had talked in a clipped language of their own, infuriating other people by their mutual telepathy. Now he knew they were asking the same question.

She slurred it into words. 'Where could he have gone when he . . . where *is* . . . ?'

In the canal, he thought. Or the culverts above the canal.

Not on the railway line, or it would have been reported by now. Perhaps lying behind a bush, perhaps drifting with the slow current. At any minute someone might come across the body and call the police, and the police would check, and soon there'd be a ring at the doorbell.

It was high time they notified the police themselves.

But without showing Harold's vindictive farewell lines, explaining what had happened and why it had happened.

Arlene said abruptly: 'There was another letter.'

'Another one?'

'I remember. He asked Amanda for three stamps.'

'Who's got it, then?' Crumpled paper whispered between his fingers. 'Who got the third letter?'

3

Inspector Brewer's dull grey eyes were darkening with suspicion. The fact that he didn't know what to suspect did nothing to lessen the suspicion. He said:

'You still haven't made it clear why you think Mr. Grant committed suicide, sir.'

Without a corpse and with their only evidence in those letters, which couldn't possibly be produced, they were in a spot.

Norman glowered at a map on the wall behind the desk. Where the hell had Harold gone and done it?

Arlene said; 'My husband has been acting very strangely recently.'

'In what way, madam?'

'He has been extremely depressed.'

'I often get that way myself, the things I'm faced with.'

Arlene sat stiff-backed on a wooden chair, her head steady against the wintry light through the police station window. In the yard outside a motorcycle was being revved up. At each snort it was answered by the anguished bark of a far-off dog. Arlene said:

'The collapse of Interflow Consultants was a great blow to him.'

'He'd still got a job. And a home. If he'd been going to do anything silly, wouldn't it have been more likely six months ago, rather than now?'

'It seemed to weigh on his mind. I know he . . . found it hard to go on.'

'You mean he talked of — well, doing something drastic?'

'Not in so many words.'

'But you had a hunch?'

'I was his wife,' said Arlene levelly. 'I knew him.'

The inspector's lips stayed set in a thin straight line. 'You and Mr. Leggett were involved with the same company. It didn't hit you too hard?'

Norman broke in. 'Towards the end we had concentrated on other activities. When the crash came, we did all we could to help, of course.'

'And you didn't take it too tragically?'

'Business,' — Norman forced a wry

grin — 'is a rough business.'

There was no acknowledging smile. 'Could he have had a nervous breakdown — wandered off in a daze?'

'No,' said Arlene.

'People do it every day, Mrs. Grant. By the thousand. You'd be amazed the way they roll up at police stations all over the country, every day, saying they've forgotten who they are.'

'Nobody could imagine Harold doing that.'

'You can imagine suicide,' said the inspector, 'but not a nervous breakdown?'

Harold bristled. 'Inspector, we've come to you in order to find . . . him. We've told you all we know.'

'And you have grounds for believing it's suicide.'

'It's a feeling we've got.' Arlene lowered her gaze. 'A dreadful feeling.' Norman nodded affirmation.

'But he left no note?'

'No.'

'They usually do.'

'Not a word.'

'Look, Mrs. Grant. Sir. Do you know

how many people go missing in this country every year? Twenty to thirty thousand. Every year. Some just lose their memory: just seem to chuck it away as though they couldn't be bothered with it any more, and off they go. Others . . . ' He permitted himself a pseudo-deferential glance at Arlene. 'Others,' he said, 'just clear off anyway. Decide they can't stand any more domestic bliss, or what have you. And,' — before Arlene could interrupt — 'it's not a criminal offence, and it's not our job to trace them.'

'It's a disgrace,' said Norman.

'Twenty thousand of them. Thirty thousand. Unless you have evidence of something criminal — enough to justify the coroner authorising us to start looking — then all we can do is put him on our register of missing persons. And sit back and wait.' The inspector took their silence as submission, and said more amiably: 'We'll circulate a description. A recent photograph would help.'

Arlene said: 'I don't think we've got anything recent.'

'No holiday snaps?'

'We haven't bothered with that sort of thing for years.'

The inspector's mouth showed emotion at last. Its ends turned sourly down. He said: 'Well, anything you can rustle up. And I'll get a man in and you can dictate a description of Mr. Grant. Particularly what he was wearing on Thursday night.'

Description of the clothes was easy enough. Harold himself was a tougher proposition. His limp was his only distinguishing feature, and to the casual observer even that could appear a mannerism rather than an affliction.

'You know how it is,' said Norman. 'Brown hair, brown eyes, clean-shaven, medium height, ordinary sort of voice. Doesn't help much, does it?'

'There really isn't anything special to say, Inspector,' Arlene added.

'And who knows him better than you do?' If there was an offensive irony in the remark, it was impossible to detect it in the flat, matter-of-fact tone.

Brewer saw them to the door of the station, past a desk sergeant who watched them without raising his eyes. They went out into the bleak February morning and crossed the street to Norman's Jaguar. Brewer stood at the top of the steps until they had driven away.

'All those fiddling descriptions!' Arlene fumed. 'What good will they do? I couldn't think of one single thing to say.'

'The clothes,' said Norman. 'They'll come in useful. When they do find him, the clothes'll identify him right away.'

Arlene sank deeper into the seat. After a moment or two of staring sullenly ahead, she turned for a look at her brother. He returned her gaze. They both snorted ruefully, in unison.

'I never realised he felt that bad,' she said.

'Bloody little prig.' A dog darted into the road, he swerved, somebody blared a horn at him. It triggered his rage. 'He planned the whole thing this way, you know. Down to the last little detail. Making sure we were left in a mess, not knowing how to tidy it all up or where or . . . or . . . Did it just to spite us!' he blazed.

Arlene laughed.

He shot her another glance, no longer a shared one: they were no longer in phase. 'You think it's funny, this mess?'

The car was turning up the hill between the pub and the pillar box when Arlene said quietly: 'Something else that might amuse Harold, if he's haunting us.'

'What?'

'What that inspector's thinking. Or thinking about thinking, anyway.'

He didn't understand. Then, as he drew up on the driveway by her front door, he did understand. 'Now, wait a minute. He's not going to suspect us of — '

'Isn't he?'

'When the body turns up, they're bound to see that death was self-inflicted.'

'We hope.'

'They're not complete idiots, you know.'

'And if the body never does turn up?'

'If there's no corpse,' said Norman, getting out and waiting for her to walk round the bonnet towards him, 'they can hardly accuse us of murder.'

'I've read of cases where that happened. There was that woman in Wimbledon they never did find, but that didn't stop the police, and the judge and jury — '

'That was a weird one.'

'So's this.'

'Oh, for God's sake.'

They went into the house.

★ ★ ★

His wife was waiting for them. She wore a wine-dark sweater scalloped like a vase about her long, slim neck, and loose slacks tucked into fur-lined boots. She stood in the centre of Arlene's sitting room drinking Arlene's gin from one of Arlene's deepbowled Moser glasses. It was not her first glassful. She swayed gently, rhythmically, like a delicately balanced pendulum.

'How did you get here?' Norman demanded.

'In the Mini. How else?' Her milky mauve eyes, as cloudy as diluted Pernod, looked away from him, at Arlene. 'You never come to see me nowadays.'

'Ron, with all that's been happening — with what Arlene's going through right now, how you can — '

'She didn't come to see me for ages before that. So I thought I'd drop in. See if I could help. Amanda let me in, bless her.'

'And who let you into the booze cupboard?' Norman reached for the glass in her hand. Veronica's slender, violet-veined fingers tightened and she edged backwards.

'Arlene doesn't keep everything locked up,' she said. 'Not like at home. She doesn't mind her visitors pouring themselves a welcome, do you, Arlene?'

'Let's all sit down,' said Arlene.

A faint distant plop, felt rather than heard, signalled the time switch turning on the central heating furnace again. From upstairs a cassette player shrilled, wandering and wavering as though Amanda were drifting from room to room with it.

Norman said: 'You don't mind that awful racket at a time like this?'

'I've no intention of putting Amanda in a veil and black armband, and telling her to meditate.'

'Even so — '

'Children get over things,' said Veronica.

'Then they find they're not children any more. It's all such a rush.' She jangled her glass down on an oak stool beside the couch and sprawled back, closing her eyes.

Norman had married her when those restless eyes had been vivid rather than vague. The translucent skin drawn sleek over her cheekbones had flushed then with easy excitement, before alcohol blotched it with a hectic dryness. He had married her because of the glow about her — a sexy halo, laughter let loose, something you couldn't fight free of once you'd come within range. She had been his secretary — not a good secretary, but a gorgeous fluttering bird to have around. She had adored his fast car and his dirty jokes; took noisy possession of the wine bars where he met his friends, appropriated his friends as her own, and didn't so much tag along with him as goad him from one experience to another. When they married she saw no reason why the tempo and atmosphere shouldn't continue as before. She was one of the gang, she could drink and swap low stories with the best of them: her fey, fragile

58

appearance added flavour to the outrageous things she loved to say.

But Norman was already moving on. It was his new subordinates who took over the drinking and the trivial little deals: at his level he no longer needed that kind of contact.

Now there came the hours at home when, at the old familiar times, she felt like a drink. And drank alone. Until she found that she was happier with it, or at any rate less lonely, if she forgot the set times and got a bottle out whenever she felt like it.

Her wispy body was provocative and rarely still. But the halo became hazed. Her fingertips were harsh, and arid patches flaked from her arms and across her stomach. The delicate blue tracery behind her face thickened into a straggling network of inner bruises.

They had no children.

He said: 'Why don't you push off home and lie down?'

Veronica's eyes remained shut. 'Why should I want to lie down?'

'Arlene and I have a lot to discuss.'

'I can listen. It's all in the family, isn't it? High time I was told what's going on.'

'Look, you know perfectly well — '

'I know poor Harold's dead. That's all I do know.' One tear squeezed itself out from under her right eyelid and trickled a couple of inches down her cheek. She screwed up her eyes as though to stop any more escaping. 'What I don't know is what you're proposing to do about it.'

'That's what we want to discuss.'

'I'm listening.'

'None of it concerns you.'

'My sweet, everything about you concerns me.'

Arlene tensed. 'Veronica, you sound very positive about Harold being dead.'

'But he is. We all know that.'

'Do we?'

'What else have you two been talking about these last few days? Dashing to and fro, plotting away on the telephone — '

'You've been snooping again,' said Norman.

'Couldn't help overhearing. Every time I've picked up the extension you've been hard at it.'

'Why are you so sure?' Arlene persisted.

Norman stared at his wife. She opened her eyes slyly, but only so that she could establish where her glass was and reach for it. It was empty.

Arlene said: 'Would you like a — '

'No, she wouldn't,' said Norman. He thrust himself up from his chair and stood over Veronica. 'Ron, did you get a letter from Harold?'

'A letter?' She still looked sly, but it was a characteristic expression nowadays, it could mean thirst or a sour private joke or nothing. 'Why would Harold ever have bothered to write to poor little me?'

'You're so certain he's dead.'

'So are you. Both of you. You told me so.'

'I never told you any such thing. All I said was that Harold had disappeared, and we were afraid he'd done something silly.'

'Well, then?'

'I said he might be dead, but I didn't say he was.'

'We all know,' said Veronica.

'How?'

He yelled it at her. She flinched. Once she would have rowed with him and then dissolved into laughter: the two kinds of screaming had been very close then. Now his voice stung like a lash tearing at her papery skin; and she flinched.

'I can tell. Harold and I were very close.'

'Oh, come off it.'

'Closer than you ever realised. I can feel . . . ' Her free hand pressed into her stomach, the hand on the glass raised in a shaky valediction. 'Anyway,' she said with abrupt joy in her own acuteness, 'there was all that stuff about veils and armbands.'

'Did you get a letter?' Norman pounded the words out.

She let her eyelids droop again.

'Leave her alone, Norman,' said Arlene. 'You're only stirring it up. We're not going to make any sense out of it this way.

He wanted to grab Veronica and shake her, shake her until those brittle bones and protruding shoulder blades all rattled together. Then he gave in. There wasn't really anything there. She was talking,

talking, the way she always did. He said:

'Come on, Ron, I'll run you home.'

'I'll leave when I'm good and ready. I drove here. I can drive home.'

'You can't. You're not fit to drive. I'm going to take you home, and you can go and lie down.'

'Lie down?' Her eyes opened, disconcertingly bright and venomous. 'All this talk about lying down. D'you hear, Arlene? He wants to rush me home and put me to bed. Or take me to bed — you're going to come with me, love?'

Over her head Norman said: 'I'll give you a ring when I've checked off — '

'He's so funny,' Veronica's voice sank to a musing malice. 'In bed, I mean. Especially in the morning. To see him stretched out there in the morning — really, he's a hoot. Honestly. Have I ever told you, Arlene — '

'Yes,' said Arlene.

'If he wasn't so funny,' — the tears flowed in full spate, the facile maudlin tears of drink rather than anguish — 'he'd be an out-and-out louse. But he really is funny. I mean, so funny. A scream.'

'Shut up and come along,' said Norman.

'And speaking of a louse . . . You know, that's what hurt Harold most. I could tell. I never interfered. You can never say I interfered, never. Neither of you. You can't say that. But I knew when he was hurt and what was hurting.' The wide unblinking eyes were staring straight back at Norman.

'And if anyone should know, it's me, isn't it? Only you haven't driven me as far as you drove Harold — not yet.'

A wild notion crossed his mind. He dismissed it, and it crept back. There was a tenuous picture of Harold and Veronica at Christmas and Harold and Veronica at Arlene's birthday party, when Norman took them all to that pub near Hatfield: Harold taking Veronica's arm, being gentle and attentive, flirting mildly and bringing the sort of smile to her lips that Norman hadn't been able to raise for some years. Not that he'd felt any inclination.

But that was all it had been — a mild flirtation within the family, strictly for

64

giggles, a sort of Christmas and birthday ritual. Like kissing all and sundry under the mistletoe.

'Harold hated parasites,' said Veronica. 'Remember how you pretended to go along with him, those early days? Eliminate the parasites, every last blood-sucking one of them. All the scroungers and hangers-on. Brave new world! The country was going to be cleaned up, we'd all be cleaner, and we'd all live happy ever after.'

'He was a sentimental nit,' said Norman, sick and fed up with Harold and everything to do with him.

'Yes, he was. Sentimental. And a nit — a parasite, because you lured him into becoming one, and . . . and . . . poor Harold,' she wept, 'he couldn't take it.'

'Come on home,' said Norman.

She was just capable of getting to her feet. When she swayed, willing herself to fall into the comatose state, which was the nearest thing to comfort she knew, he grabbed her. His hand clutched her wrist. Once she was steady, he let his hand slide up to the fabric of her sleeve.

'That's it,' she murmured. 'You don't like touching, do you?'

'Home. Right now.'

'You both hate it. The Leggett allergy — can't bear to be touched.' Her bleary gaze encompassed Arlene. 'Poor Harold.'

Norman steered her towards the door.

Arlene said soothingly: 'Once this beastly business is out of the way, we must — '

'I must just pop into the loo.'

Veronica went into the small cloakroom opening off the hall. Norman said in an undertone: 'She hasn't got a bottle in there, has she?'

'Not unless she brought it with her.'

'I wouldn't put it past her.' Weariness and rage tussled within him. 'That letter,' he said. 'That other letter.'

'You don't really think she might have been the one?'

'It doesn't make sense. What could he have had to write to Ron? Unless he got sloppy and sentimental right at the last. Fond farewells and all that. But I don't really think so. Not really.'

'A real suicide note,' Arlene breathed, 'without any mention of business.'

'That's too much to hope for.'

'If only it was as simple as that.' She was imploring her dead husband to have been unfaithful, to have been sloppy and sentimental, to have been anything that would help them now. 'At least we'd know where we are. Instead of wondering where and how and — '

'Why the hell,' Norman exploded, 'didn't he shove his head in the gas oven where we could find him?'

Veronica came out of the cloakroom fastidiously rubbing her hands together. 'Arlene doesn't have gas, do you, dear?' she said. 'She cooks by electricity.'

★　★　★

The bank manager's office throbbed with the pulsation of traffic even with its double windows shut against cold and the main road. Every few minutes the room was shadowed by double-decker buses slowing in a queue of traffic.

'The matter is a delicate one,' said Mr. Cooke. 'Death isn't a thing you can take for granted.'

Norman had always favoured yes-no situations. You did a deal or you didn't. You went full steam ahead or you cut your losses and called the whole thing off.

And here he was floundering on an unfathomable mud bank.

'But how long do we have to wait?'

'Before you can presume death?'

'Yes.'

'As a general rule,' said Cooke, 'seven years.'

'Seven years!'

'Unless you have incontrovertible evidence of death, which I'm sure we all hope you don't get.' He was more unctuous than Inspector Brewer, because the Pledge and Distraint Services account was an important one; but there was a flickering echo of Brewer's doubts behind his cautious responses. 'Until every other avenue has been explored, I don't see that such a presumption can be accepted. Legally accepted,' he stressed.

'It puts us in a most unsatisfactory position,' said Norman.

'It does indeed, Mr. Leggett. But I'm afraid that all you can do is carry on your side of the business as before, and wait until something turns up.'

'Something?' Norman had the latest in a succession of visions — Harold floating to the surface of the canal halfway across Buddinghamshire (or did the current flow the other way?), or decomposing beneath a hawthorn bush, or being dug up a hundred years from now by a plough, or whatever they'd be using a hundred years from now.

Cooke said: 'I suppose there is no likelihood that . . . um . . . because of some misconception . . . ' He stopped. The necessity for tact in what was a personal rather than a straightforward financial matter snarled up his tongue. 'It simply doesn't seem credible to me,' he said with a surge of hopeful joviality, 'but could Mr. Grant have been impetuous enough to desert Mrs. Grant — even if only temporarily?'

'No,' said Norman flatly.

'These things do happen.'

People are doing it every day . . .

Bloody parrot.

Norman said: 'You can imagine how

upsetting this is for my sister.'

'Indeed I can. Do convey my deepest sympathies to her.'

'I'll do that.'

'And my hopes,' said Cooke, 'that there'll be a happy ending soon. I'm sure we'll see Mr. Grant back home in no time at all.'

Mr. Grant, Norman announced firmly and silently into the unknown, is dead. Somewhere or other. Mr. flaming creepy lousy little Harold Grant is dead — and has mucked up his death the way he mucked up his life.

'The house,' he said. 'And the insurance policy my sister holds. It's all the waiting that's so worrying. The uncertainty.'

'I appreciate that.'

'The executors have the right to call in the full sum I owe on that house.'

'On presumption of death.'

'That's what I'm saying. I don't know where I am.'

'Until we have definite news to the contrary — which I sincerely hope we don't get — we may safely assume that Mr. Grant is still alive. The position remains as it was. And since you were kind enough to advise Mr. Grant to appoint this bank as executor,' said Cooke blandly, 'I don't foresee any real problems, whatever may happen. If any should arise, I trust you won't hesitate to approach me.'

'I'd just like to have the whole situation settled.'

'So would we all. Now, if Mr. Grant has been unfortunate enough to have a temporary aberration — a fit of amnesia, say — '

'You've been talking to the police.'

Cooke permitted himself a shocked reproof. 'It would never occur to me to talk to the police or anyone else about the affairs of our clients.'

'Amnesia!' said Norman bitterly. 'The police have got that one on the brain, too.'

'It does seem a strong possibility.'

'Not to me it doesn't. Or to Mrs. Grant.'

Cooke seemed lost for a reply. He shuffled some papers on his desk, and looked up thankfully as there was a tap at the door.

'Come in.'

A girl put her head timidly into the room. 'I'm sorry to interrupt, Mr. Cooke, but Mr. Aylmer thought you ought to see something that's just come in.'

'I do have somebody with me,' the manager chided.

'Mr. Aylmer says it's something . . .' She glanced apprehensively at Norman. 'You might find it useful, he says, in what you're dealing with.'

'Indeed?' Cooke had welcomed the interruption but now disapproved. The moment of relief had been in contravention of regulations that he had established. He stood up and shook his head apologetically at Norman. 'I really am most sorry about this. It had better be important.'

He readjusted his face from the expression suitable for dealing with a client to that most appropriate for his staff.

'Won't keep you a minute,' he said, and strode out.

Norman glowered at the calendar. Another Tuesday had come round. Two more fruitless interviews with the police, and two advertisements, which they had felt compelled to put into *The Times* and the local paper — and not a flicker of news. Not that he had expected any direct response. But each day he had thought that today or tomorrow the body would be found. Or the next day. Now twelve had gone.

Showing the bank manager those blasted letters would surely put an end to his doubts. Harold's intention had been plainly, irrevocably stated. Unfortunately a lot of other things had been stated just as plainly. Even with those profitable Pledge and Distraint accounts to consider, the manager could hardly overlook Harold's revelations. The curt summary of that currency fiddle on behalf of the tour operating company they had tidied up; and the Notting Hill property deal where Norman had found a fast way of evicting fifty tenants who'd been stubborn about their rent and then setting up a plushy new deal for the client: no, none of it would amuse a bank manager or a rents tribunal.

Or the coroner.

It suddenly hit him. Could Harold, in one last malicious fling, have sent that third letter to old Jefferson?

The heat of the electric radiators scorched Norman's left cheek and jaw. A cold draught from one ill-fitting corner of the window chilled the side of his neck.

Jefferson would be the one to hold the inquest. And Jefferson hated him. That bit of trouble with two fellow Masons which led to Norman quitting the Lodge had turned out for the best, really: it had been a bit embarrassing using strong-arm methods of collecting debts from two laggard brothers. But Jefferson hadn't forgiven him. And Jefferson as coroner could say and hint whatever he liked.

You had no redress. Coroners were worse than judges when it came to splashing personal prejudices around.

Produce the letters. Brazen it out. Say how upsetting it all was, how warped poor Harold must have been in his last tragic moments. Balance of his mind seriously disturbed.

He could almost hear what Jefferson would make of that.

Outside, a car's brakes shrieked. It stalled. The driver had to have four tries before it would start again. There was a protracted whine, cut into by a salvo of blaring horns.

He was desperate to get the pieces swept up. Then back to work.

Could they plant some evidence? Scatter a few things near the canal to show where Harold had fallen in.

And when they dragged it and didn't find him . . . ?

Fake his handwriting, produce a nice convincing suicide note. Arlene could identify the handwriting: it would be hard to shake her testimony.

Cooke came back into the room.

'Well,' he said heavily. 'Well.' He was slapping a small wad of cheques against his left palm. 'You're right about one thing, Mr. Leggett. It certainly doesn't look like a case of amnesia.'

Norman began to get up. 'You've heard something?'

Cooke turned the uppermost cheque towards him, 'You recognise that signature?'

The name was Harold Grant's. The ink was the rusty black ink Harold always used in his fountain pen. The handwriting was Harold's.

He couldn't speak.

'Your brother-in-law,' said Cooke, 'drew a new cheque-book on the Tuesday before he . . . disappeared. There were thirty cheques in it. Every one of them was filled in and cashed in one day.'

'Which day?'

'Last Friday. It usually takes three days for such cheques to go up to the clearing house and then be sent on to us. This time we've had the weekend to add to it.'

'But what does it mean?'

'It would appear to mean,' said Cooke austerely, 'that Mr. Grant was still alive last Friday, and by no means suffering from loss of memory.'

'Sixty cheques — '

'Thirty. When his company cheque-book was withdrawn after the bankruptcy, he had only the personalised cheques. We make up the books only in thirties nowadays. And,' — Cooke was taking advantage of this golden opportunity to deliver a lecture — 'we permitted that only because I had your personal guarantee of backing for Mr. Grant should any . . . ah . . . unpleasant circumstances arise.'

'Thirty cheques. How much was drawn altogether?'

'The maximum permissible,' said Cooke, 'against his thirty-pound bank card.'

'Nine hundred quid.'

'Precisely.'

'I didn't realise you could cash a whole book at one go, against that card.'

'Not all at one go. But there's nothing to stop you from dashing between different branches and collecting several lots of thirty in an hour or two. Mr. Grant appears to have moved fast — and far. He started in Coventry.' Cooke riffled through the wad, nodding confirmation of the sequence. 'Probably he hired a car. He chose large conurbations with three or four branches not too far apart, and drew thirty pounds at each.' He extracted two cheques and studied them. 'Mm. Didn't have to stick to our own branches — our card is valid at all the major banks.'

'Why choose the Midlands rather than London?'

'Perhaps he didn't want to bump into

anyone he knew. Your organisation does cover a large part of London. He couldn't risk being slowed down. He was obviously anxious' — Cooke grew even more solemn and censorious — 'to acquire as much as possible in that one day, before anyone caught up with him.'

'Why wait until last Friday? Why not cash in quick the week before, the day after he disappeared?'

Cooke shrugged. 'I really couldn't say.'

Norman thought of that hopeless plan he had half dreamed up only a few minutes ago. If Harold's signature could be forged on a letter, why not on a cheque? But of course: much easier on a cheque, in fact, when you had a helpful specimen in front of you.

He burst out: 'It wasn't Harold!'

Cooke, startled, held up the cheques at eye level.

'No!' cried Norman. 'Not Harold at all! Don't you see?'

'I must confess that what I see is unmistakably Mr. Grant's signature.'

'But that's where you're wrong. It's always struck me as one of the dangers of this personalised stuff — any crook who lays his hand on the cheque-book and the card at the same time is home and dry. All he has to do is practise the signature from the card, and then cash in.'

'A convincing forgery isn't as easy as all that.'

'But given time . . . time!' Norman exulted. 'That's why there was a week's delay. Whoever stole Harold's new cheque-book and card must have been practising. Taking his time, making sure he got it right. And then grabbing the lot all in one day and clearing off.'

'Stealing Mr. Grant's pen also?'

'His pen, his wallet — the lot, I'd guess. He'd have helped himself to anything he could, and then . . . and then hidden the body. That's why we haven't found it. It explains everything.'

Cooke edged an uneasy step backwards. 'Mr. Leggett, you do seem remarkably keen to believe that Mr. Grant is dead.'

'Keen? No such thing. But we have to face facts.'

'Which facts? You seem so sure Mr. Leggett was in a suicidal mood that night.

Isn't it even likelier — if these cheques are forged, as you claim — that he was attacked and robbed? Killed by mistake, perhaps, in the struggle.'

It was plausible. Denying it would put him in an odd light. 'It could be,' he conceded. 'But — '

'But likelier still,' purred Cooke, who didn't often get a half-hour of this calibre, 'that Mr. Grant simply walked out on his wife and family, drew as much money as he was able to, and settled down wherever it was he had in mind.'

'That's a monstrous suggestion.'

'Basically no more monstrous than walking out the other way — by death.'

Norman could have struck him then and there. He was in great need of someone to bash. Possibly Cooke had sensed this when he saw fit to back away.

Norman said: 'It's no part of your job to put forward theories on personal matters.'

'No.' Cooke drew himself up. 'No, that's quite true. I was merely trying to clear things up to our mutual satisfaction.' The cheques slapped once more against his left palm. 'But this isn't a personal matter. This concerns the bank. In view of our — ah — speculations this morning, I must say I'd like to find out exactly what is going on.'

And you're not the only one, thought Norman savagely.

Harold's tidy black signature mocked him. It couldn't possibly be genuine. And yet . . .

Where was Harold? Harold, dead or alive; murdered, self-destroyed, or a deserter. And if dead, what had the robber done with the corpse and where was he now: the real Harold or the forger, which was he and where was he?

4

The sea had been pounding from the north-east for two days, thrust on by an unrelenting wind. At night ships lay in the shelter of the promontory enclosing the bay north of Ormeswich, their lights spangling the dark inseparable sea and sky. At ten-second intervals the cold yet comforting beam of the lighthouse scythed the wave crests.

This morning the wind had slackened. In the lull, most of the ships turned out towards the open sea. By late afternoon the vane on top of the lighthouse was veering south-east, and long rollers came rhythmically over the shore. A dark rash of pebbles pockmarked the sand. Driftwood littered the tide-line. The horizon was sullen mauve edged by a steel-grey gleam. A few hours of this swell would scour the pebbles out again and toss the driftwood into new patterns and new places.

Judith Marshall went down the steps to the narrow concrete promenade and walked towards the close-set thumbs, one white and one flinty, of lighthouse and church tower.

She was thirty-two, slim, and only just on five feet six inches, though the high-peaked hood she was wearing made her look taller. Her legs were rather solid, so she often wore corduroy slacks — they were a comfort for most of the year in Ormeswich, anyway — and she had always envied girls with slender, fine-boned ankles. 'Legs like that,' her father had said, 'she ought to be a rugger player.' He had said it affectionately and approvingly, but she had never liked it.

She had the slightly sandy fairness and bright complexion, which the Dutch and the Danes had brought through the centuries to this coast.

Her hood was attached by press-studs to a woollen cloak, which Jim had brought from Antwerp five years ago, only a few weeks before the North Sea claimed him once and for all. The green-trimmed cloak and the fur hood were her constant shield against the raw easterlies.

Even on a winter's day like this she liked to use the promenade, only a few feet above high water mark. It was somehow warmer down here under the low cliffs than up in the town. There were too many draughty corners and too many flurries of cold air between the road where she lived and the school on the far side of the church. Besides, in the town nothing much changed: on the rare occasions when a shop window display was rearranged, the new formation was the same as before only more so. The same cars and mud-spattered vans were parked outside the same chosen pubs each morning. In the afternoon the usual predictable ladies would emerge from Peddars Place with their usual cohorts of poodles and dachshunds — three or four to a leash, sometimes — to foul their favourite parts of pavement a suitable distance from Peddars Place.

The sea was never the same two days in succession; or five minutes in succession. The hills and gullies of the shore were always restless, always new.

Judith heard the school bus grind out of its shed on the road above, and quickened her pace. Peter would be out in ten minutes.

She studied the trim row of beach chalets.

Their spiky wooden elegance softened the harshness of the concrete and preserved some of Ormeswich's tidy Edwardian charm. Born and brought up here, knowing the owners of most of the chalets and of the more sprawling shacks in the sand dunes, Judith still had a vision of one of those doors opening one day and a moustachioed man in long striped bathing costume striding out to the encouraging strains of a military band on the pier. Only Ormeswich no longer had a pier: it had been blown up early in the Second World War.

As she approached she realised that one of the doors was in fact open.

At this time of year the chalets ought to be unoccupied. The town council cut off water supplies to the rear of the huts between October and the beginning of May, and there was a by-law against

85

anyone cooking there or sleeping there during that period. A few amateur fisher-men kept their rods there, and would bait up on Sunday morning in the shelter of the arched veranda. Otherwise they should be bolted and shuttered.

A shutter hung loose. One door swung inwards on its hinges. Two young men came out, and said something to someone inside.

Then one of them saw Judith and said something short and explosive to his companion.

They both laughed aggressively — about nothing.

Judith hesitated. She couldn't turn back now, or she would be late at the school. She walked on.

The two danced in front of her. A third came out of the chalet, at first looking the same, with the same lank hair and ragged floral waistcoat, and that sagging lip and uncommunicative grin you seemed to see everywhere nowadays. Not so much of it in the winter, as a rule: it came back, like the return of an enfeebled Cheshire cat, with the spring and summer visitors.

The third proved to be a girl. It was evident only by the way she swung her head and, instinctively, brushed her hair back with long, broken-nailed fingers.

'Did you have a good Christmas?' One of the youths jarred against Judith's elbow and blundered around her as she tried to maintain her pace.

'Goodwill,' said the girl in a giggled incantation. 'Goodwill. Goodwill — right?'

'Please,' said Judith.

They jostled her, slowed her down.

'Please what?' said one.

They brought her to a standstill. The leering vacuity of their faces enraged her. 'You've no business here.'

'If you mean we have no commercial ties with the town, we have to grant you that.'

'Got to grant her that, yes.'

'But if you mean we have no right to breathe the good fresh air — '

'You've no business in Mrs. Chadwick's beach hut.'

'So it's Mrs. Chadwick's, is it?'

'Nice name, Chadwick,' said the girl. 'I wonder if I'll ever be a Mrs. Chadwick?'

Judith said: 'You're in my way.'

'The promenade's free,' said the young man on her left.

His breath smelt of something like very sweet toffee. 'Come to sunny Ormeswich. Country walks, pretty promenade . . . gay night life . . . delightful dollies . . . It's all in the leaflet, obtainable from the town hall. Please enclose one unused postage stamp for reply.'

She felt one of them lean against her elbow again, and she jabbed it sharply into his side.

'Oh, now, that's nasty. Peace is what we support. Dirty fighting doesn't suit us.'

They began their mocking dance again. It was meaningless. She knew it didn't matter and that there was nothing to be afraid of. They came and went, these pathetic little groups — shoved contemptuously out by the police, or just drifting off from sheer inability to find anything that amused them. All the same it was frightening.

The parade above was set back a few feet from the grassy edge of the cliff, and the roofs of the chalets masked this stretch of promenade. And not many people used the seaward side of the parade on a day like this, anyway: they tended to hug the far side of the road and scuttle indoors at the earliest opportunity.

There couldn't be any real violence. There wasn't, ever, in Ormeswich. A few drunks, a few louts on motorbikes: they came and went, never stuck it for long.

But her heart quickened.

'Please,' she said. 'I have to hurry. I've got to get to school.'

'A bit late to start learning things, isn't it?'

'I gave up long ago,' the girl giggled.

'You mean they gave you up.'

The three of them bumped together in mutual appreciation. Judith hurried on, hoping they would forget her.

But they began to run after her.

Below the promenade the shore curved outwards now and rose to the low barrier of sand dunes. A few shacks and more substantial holiday houses were built up on thick, squat stilts rising from the marram grass.

Someone was stumbling across the

sand from one of them, a converted smokehouse. Not another of this dismal gang? Judith heard a sob break from her throat, and was ashamed and even more furious than before. When the youth who had started it all caught up and screeched and dodged in front of her, she hit him with all her might across the face.

The other two screeched and caught her arms.

The man on the shore reached the promenade, and his feet scrabbled on the shingle as he jumped up. He rocked perilously on the edge of the concrete for a moment, then braced himself and came on.

'Hey, look, you . . . '

The girl's warning was too late. The newcomer grabbed one young man's arm with his right hand and seemed to duck and turn half right. Off balance, the young man swung almost over in a descending arc. His cheek struck the concrete and travelled a good three or four feet along it. A dull red stain like smeared ink followed him.

Judith was conscious of the second youth reeling away, flailing his arms. A fist struck up below his guard; his head went back, and the edge of a palm hammered under his nose once, twice, three times. He whimpered and crumpled.

The girl cried: 'You bastard. You dirty, rotten — '

'Rubbish,' said the man crisply. He rubbed the knuckles of his right hand into his left palm and said to Judith: 'I'll see you to the end of the promenade.'

'I . . . thank you, I . . . think I'll be all right now.'

'So do I,' he said with a short, bubbling laugh.

She had been frightened by the trio; grateful for his intervention; and yet wasn't sure that he wasn't the more frightening. It had all been so quick. And ruthless. The man had enjoyed it — had known what he was doing and done it fast and viciously.

She said: 'I'm awfully glad you were there.'

Instinctively she looked out towards the huddle of buildings in the dunes. Like the chalets, they were usually deserted until the warmer weather brought tourists and weekenders back.

'Don't worry,' he said cheerfully. 'I'm not like that little lot. I've a right to be there. Renting the place from the Drabbles.'

Drabble and Drabble were the Ship Street estate agents, doing most of their trade in summer lets and maintenance of holiday houses. Judith said:

'They must have been surprised to have a customer so early this year.'

'Very reasonable,' he said. 'The whole place is booked up after Easter, but they let me have that shack at a reduced rent till then.'

'You like it cold and lonely?'

'I can do with a spell of that.'

She wondered what had driven him here. He wasn't a local, he didn't look like the regulars who came loyally back time after time; he belonged somewhere else — and remembering that practised savagery, she couldn't think it had much in common with faded, phlegmatic Ormeswich.

'Until Easter,' she said politely.

'That's right.'

They reached the steps at the end of the promenade, and she held out her hand.

'Thank you again.'

He took her hand. She could hardly repress a shiver at the strength of his grip — a grip that had overthrown two young men half his age in a matter of seconds.

She climbed to the paved lookout beside the church wall. The road to the school swung twenty or thirty yards inland and curled round the churchyard. Most people took the well-trodden path between the flowering shrubs and the salt-scoured gravestones.

Glancing back just once, she saw her rescuer plod back across the land towards the smokehouse. He, too, looked back once: at the church tower so near the cliff edge, or the lighthouse, or herself, it was impossible to say.

Peter came out of school, as usual, with his hair in a tangle, his shirt half out of his trousers, and a large dirty mark down one sleeve, which wasn't his fault, it really wasn't, he was absolutely sure of that although he wasn't sure how it had happened. For a few steps she kept her hand on his shoulder and pulled him close, and he rubbed his head into her side; then he tugged away and walked on his own, swinging his satchel and humming to himself.

'What did you have for lunch?'

'Something.'

'I'm sure you did. But what sort of something?'

'Mince, I think,' he said indifferently. Then: 'Yes, it was mince all right. It was rotten.'

'You ate it all up?'

'Oh, Mum. Honest. I had two helpings of the pudding, anyway.'

'What was that?'

'I don't remember, but it was all right.'

They went back through the town. It was getting dark already, and she didn't want to risk the promenade again. She stopped to buy a packet of fish fingers; and Peter's pace slowed, he dawdled, looking at boxes of games in the toy and sports shop window.

'Come on,' she urged. 'I've got a pupil the minute we get home.'

The pupil was a resentful girl who was mad on horses and hated the piano. Her parents were horsey types themselves, but had decided it would be a good thing for her to learn the piano: they maintained their resolution in spite of eighteen months of slam-bang practising and regular fits of tantrums.

Judith closed her eyes as the girl's stubby fingers crashed up and down a series of arpeggios. Then she opened them again: the noise was worse when you concentrated.

Music had ceased to be music to her. She rarely listened now, as she and Jim had listened once, to broadcast concerts. It was a matter now of mathematics, no more: counting the wrong notes, counting the beats, adding up the fees at the end of each week and working out food and heat and light bills.

'No, Melanie — you're still striking that semitone every time! One-and-two-and . . . one-two-three . . . Don't rush it. Don't plod. Do take your foot off the loud pedal. Doh-ray-me-fah-so-lah-te . . . No, you difficult little . . . No, not the B flat, the . . . yes, that's it: te . . . doh.'

If music be the food of love.

Not love. Just food.

When the child had gone she gave Peter his tea. An hour and a half later she presented Major Kendrick with a meal that they referred to as dinner, though it would have been more appropriate to call it early supper.

As she cleared away afterwards he sat there for five minutes, telling her again what a wonderful cook she was and how she spoiled him, and then asked how Peter was getting on at school and where she thought of sending him later. 'Could always put in a word for him at Sandhurst. Though I don't know any of the chaps there nowadays, I suppose.' He checked his gold hunter against the mantelpiece clock. It was not a criticism of her clock or a doubt about his watch: simply part of his ritual.

'Think I might drop in at the Club for the odd hour or so.'

There had not been an evening in the three years of his residence here when he had not dropped into the Club just to see how things were going, just to see if old Fred was in, just for the odd hour or so.

He got up slowly, with the usual painful

halfway pause because of his back. Then he stiffened and marched out. His blue eyes, flecked with a few tired little runnels of red, crinkled their gentle smile as he passed her.

★   ★   ★

Two afternoons later, as she and Peter walked away from the school gates, the stranger joined them.

'Mrs. Marshall.'

'Yes, that's right.' She faltered, then kept walking. Peter looked curiously up into the man's face.

It was a face, she hazarded, in its early forties. The eyes were deep-set, and although the man smiled readily enough — quite a boyish, spontaneous grin — there was somehow an opaque mask over those brown, stubborn eyes.

He said: 'I understand you give piano lessons.'

It was unexpected. 'You're only here till Easter,' she blurted out.

He laughed, and held open the churchyard gate for her to go through.

Peter followed, saying 'Thank you,' with an answering laugh.

They walked down the flagged path and then on to the hard-trodden gravel, which cut past the tower and on between the gravestones.

'Two of my favourites.' The stranger slowed, indicating a massive raised stone box on one side, a simple headstone on the other.

On the side of the bulky monument was the legend:

Here Lieth
JOHN CRUDEN
Master Mariner
Who died Decr 14th
AD1866 aged 53
also
his loving wife
and staunch mate
MARY JANE
who did rear a
sturdy crew of
eight sons
and not one of them
on borrowed milk

The single stone declared:

In Memory of
ANGUS MCMENEMY
who did settle in
this parish when
aged 21 and did never
more wish to leave it
until
God did so command
on his 80th birthday
being the 17th day of
April 1812

'I'm already beginning to think of them as personal friends.'

'Have you seen inside?' asked Peter suddenly.

'Not yet. I keep promising myself — '

'But you ought to.' Peter seized his hand and tried to turn him back towards the church.

Judith said: 'Peter, this gentleman doesn't want — '

'Pearson,' said the stranger.

'Mr. Pearson doesn't want — '

'But I'd love to see inside. It's always

better in the company of someone who knows what he's talking about.'

They went in below the chequered flushwork of the south porch. Before the war there had been Victorian stained glass in the east window and some of the windows of the north aisle. A hit-and-run raider scurrying back to base had ditched a stick of bombs that split a buttress and blew out all the windows. Today they were of plain glass, so that even on the greyest day the interior was filled with a stark radiance.

'The poppyheads, you see, show the seven deadly sins.' Peter knowledgeably patted each bench-end on its smooth, worn cranium. Avarice extended greedy arms around a huge lump of wood on which the lines of a fishing net and the heads of a few writhing fish were by now almost obliterated. Gluttony's head ripped back while the right hand fed a string of herring into its gaping mouth.

Pearson stopped below the model four-master, which hung from the roof of the nave, and craned his neck to look upwards.

'There's more of Neptune in here,' he observed, 'than any other deity.'

'And he'll probably get all the rest of it in the end,' said Peter with youthful callousness.

Judith said: 'Hundreds of years ago there were ten churches and a monastery in Ormeswich. They've all gone. The cliffs keep crumbling. This one is too close to the edge for comfort.'

Peter edged along a pew, glancing back to see if Pearson was following. He stopped below a polished brass plaque on the northern wall.

Six names were listed on the plaque. Four of them belonged to the same family.

'The lifeboat,' Pearson murmured, reading.

'Lost with all hands.'

A few inches lower, a single brass plate had been fastened more recently.

Pearson said: 'James Marshall.' He pursed his lips. 'March 1967 . . . ?'

'My dad,' said Peter.

They went out and followed the path to its end this time, emerging on to the clifftop lookout.

Judith felt that Pearson was waiting for her to add something. She said: 'They never replaced the old lifeboat. There's a light rescue boat now. James went out with two others to help an idiot in a sailing dinghy who ought never to have left harbour. Complete idiot. They got him. His boat got smashed up on the harbour groyne. And Jim was washed overboard, a long way out. They couldn't do a thing. They ought never to have been out there in that little thing.'

Pearson looked back into the church-yard as though perhaps expecting to see a newer, whiter gravestone in the middle of the hunched grey shapes.

'The cemetery's on the road out of the town nowadays,' said Judith. 'But he's not there. He was never . . . recovered.'

The tide was breaking. Thirty feet below them, a spume-topped tongue of water licked rapidly round the cluster of sand dunes, withdrew, then thrust again, further and more vigorously, towards the foot of the cliff.

'I wouldn't like to live in one of those houses there,' said Peter.

'Peter! Mr. Pearson's living there.'

'Only till Easter,' he reminded her.

They walked together into the town. Peter did a little skip as they set off and gave the newcomer a quick, shy grin. Judith was startled. It wasn't like him: he was always quiet and polite with strangers, rarely effusive. Now, somehow, there seemed to be an immediate rapport between these two. Pearson slapped the boy's shoulder very gently — not too hearty, not with any forced joviality, but as though they had known each other for years.

She found it disturbing.

For the sake of something to say, she said: 'All those churches washed away — some of the fishermen say you can still hear the bells ringing under the water.'

'And can you?'

'Of course not. But Jim did say that some nights you could see the phosphorescence of bones in the cliff face, where the old graveyards used to be.'

'Not the present one?'

'Not yet,' said Peter gleefully.

They turned out of Ship Street into High Street. Brakes squealed as a car juddered to a halt in the middle of the road. An old woman with a silver-topped cane stumped her way very slowly from one side to the other, not looking to left or right.

'She doesn't seem to fancy living much longer,' said Pearson.

'Ooh, but she does,' said Peter. 'She wants to live for ever, doesn't she, Mum?'

Judith said: 'She certainly doesn't intend to give up yet.' The arthritic but upright figure reached safety and continued its arrogant course. 'That's our Mrs. Ainsworth. She's 101.'

'If she wants to reach 102 — '

'She wants to get quite a way beyond that. There's a woman down the coast who's 104. Mrs. Ainsworth has one aim in life — to outlive her. *And* pass her.'

Major Kendrick came out of the Godyll Club with a fellow member. They stood on the step blinking. It was not a particularly bright day, but she supposed they had been bending over the snooker table for a large part of the afternoon. He saw her, raised his hat, and smiled at Peter.

Pearson had no apparent intention of leaving them.

Judith said: 'What made you ask about piano lessons?'

'I passed your house yesterday. I didn't know it was your house then, of course, but I saw you in the window and I heard someone playing scales. And when I came back that way, a lot later, somebody a bit better was practising.'

'You're not thinking of starting — '

'Not starting.' He looked from side to side, taking in the shop fronts and the names and the people who stood chatting or checking off their shopping lists. He might have been adding up, wanting to make sure that he missed nothing before working out the answer. 'I used to play, years ago. Neglected it, I'm afraid. You know how it is — have to work, make a living . . . '

'For the family,' she suggested, probing.

He said: 'What I want is the chance to play, and be told where I'm going wrong, and — well, make myself concentrate just for a little while.'

'Mum's awfully good,' said Peter. 'One chap in my form says that no matter how awful you are — '

'Peter!' To Pearson she said: 'You haven't got a piano in the place you're renting.'

'I'm afraid not.'

'Without daily practice, you're not going to get far.'

'Perhaps, as well as having lessons, I could pay you for use of your piano. From time to time. I mean, when you're not actually giving lessons.'

'It wouldn't work out very well,' she hedged.

'I can fit in with your timetable. My time,' he said, 'is my own.'

'Until Easter.'

'Yes, until Easter.'

'I can't make a virtuoso out of you by then.'

'I'd like you to bully me into some sort of achievement,' he said. 'No matter how awful I am.' He touched Peter's arm, and they both chuckled.

She felt uneasy. But the money would be welcome. If that was how he chose to spend this odd holiday of his, it was no concern of hers; she'd give him lessons, he'd leave, and if he was able to entertain the family or pals with a Chopin study or a few reasonably competent waltzes, presumably he'd feel he'd had his money's worth.

They had left the two Georgian squares of the town behind, and the picturesque fishermen's rows opening off High Street were giving way to the regularity of Ormeswich's three files of semi-detached villas, leading on to the small housing estate.

She stopped outside her house. Pearson was still with them.

He said: 'When do I start?'

'I'll have to have a look at my book.'

'Come on in,' said Peter. 'Knock out a few choruses while Mum sorts it out.'

She could hardly keep him waiting on the step. The three of them went indoors. It was colder here than outside.

She couldn't afford to have the hall heater or the gas fire in the sitting room on until they got back from school, unless she had pupils in.

'All right,' she decided abruptly. 'Sit down and play a scale in C.'

'Right now?'

'You wanted to know when you could start.'

She took her small appointments book off the shelf while he sat at the keyboard and made three false starts. They always did, no matter how advanced they were. Then, when she said nothing, he took some albums off the top of the piano and leafed through them. He began to play one of the simpler Brahms waltzes.

Judith stood behind him. His fingering was awkward. He was half-remembering patterns of fingers rather than following the music set up in front of him.

She said: 'You do have some bad habits, don't you?'

'I had a nasty feeling you were going to say that.'

She liked the way his hair bunched and threatened to curl in four different directions at once just behind his ears.

'The mornings would be better for me,' she said. 'Say ten o'clock each Wednesday?'

'Couldn't you manage a lesson every day?'

She was taken aback. 'You're that

serious about it?'

'I'd like to stick at it. Every day. And if you can hire the piano to me, as it were, when you're not using it . . . '

'You're not due to give a recital in London, or something?'

His laugh was so engaging, and yet so disturbing.

'*Will* you be able to manage it?' he said.

She leafed through the book again. 'I can manage ten o'clock three mornings a week. You can have it for practice just after lunch every day except Friday. And one of your lessons'll have to be an afternoon one.'

He spun round on the piano stool and took out his wallet.

'Shall I pay you something in advance?'

'Good heavens!'

'What's wrong?'

'Nobody round here ever does *that*,' she said ruefully. 'In fact, it's sometimes all I can do . . . '

She checked herself. Petty complaints against the tardiness of other pupils or their parents might sound too much like a heavy hint.

There was a dull booming noise coming through the wall. Glad of the diversion, she said:

'I wonder what he's watching?'

'Your lad's a television fiend?'

'He's very good about it. I let him watch some programmes, and not others. There are one or two gangster things on at this time of day — even the children's programmes go in for this thick-ear stuff — I don't want him to soak that sort of thing up.'

'It's a rough world outside,' said Pearson. There was a chill in his voice colder than the still frigid room. 'You don't think he may as well learn early on?'

'There's too much of it,' she said vaguely but angrily. 'Violence, old people getting pushed around . . . robbed . . . '

'Isn't it all robbery?' He might have been talking to himself. 'Grabbing this, grabbing that — taking from anyone who's fool enough to let you get that close?'

His wallet was open and he was looking inquiringly at her, waiting for her to say what her fee was and how much she would like now.

110

'I . . . what I usually charge,' said Judith, 'is fifty pence an hour. Just for practising, on your own, I'm not sure. I've never . . . I'll have to work it out.'

The wallet was fat with five-and ten-pound notes.

'Let's leave it at fifty for that as well,' he said.

'Oh no, I don't think I could take that.' Staring at the wad of notes, she said in what she hoped sounded like a joke: 'Talking of robbery, have you been stealing something?'

There was a moment in which she felt bleak, biting fear.

Then he said, very quietly: 'Just a few months, that's all. A few months, before I move on.'

5

This would be the last time. He'd had enough. As she wriggled against him and tugged the sheet up under his chin with a clucking noise, at the same time prodding and tickling him with her free hand, Norman knew this was another one due to be written off.

He slid out of bed and began to take his clothes from the back of the chair.

'You're not deserting me?' It was meant to be roguish and irresistible. 'Not with all the rest of the lovely morning left?'

'I've got a lot of work waiting for me.'

'I stayed in all day for you yesterday. And now — '

'I told you. I got caught up in a meeting.' In fact he had forgotten all about her until he set out this morning.

'And now,' she persevered, 'you just hop in and out as though . . . well . . . ' She peeked up at him. The roguishness simmered down. She was a bit late responding to the warning in his face; she didn't yet know just how late. 'Can't you manage it again before next week? It doesn't have to be only once a week, does it?'

Her voice crept stickily into his head, the way her hands had crept round the back of his neck that first time.

He tightened his tie in front of the wardrobe mirror. That wardrobe had no right to be here, really. It wouldn't be here much longer. Nor would the carpet. Nor would he. Not knowing when it was wise to stop, she wheedled: 'I'm beginning to think you've got some other poor woman enslaved. I'll get mad, I'm telling you. You've heard about a woman scorned, haven't you?'

'Yes.'

'I'm not good at sharing things.'

She was becoming far too possessive. The balance was shifting; and that was something he never allowed to happen.

He could pick and choose. There were so many of them running up debts without daring to let their husbands know. Nothing they wouldn't do to keep things quiet. Anything to put off the evil day. Very amenable, some of them. You had to know how to make the most of it — and know when to get out.

The early stages were the best. Especially with the ones who really hated him but had to offer themselves. Then he liked to force them into enjoying him. When they began to relish it for its own sake, and get too greedy and demanding, it became a nuisance.

Today he was impatient to reach the office.

She got out of bed and pawed a fond farewell, smacking wet kisses into his ear, which he detested.

'Next Wednesday, then?'

'Don't you think it's about time you settled that outstanding debt?'

She pouted. 'I thought we'd forgotten all that beastly business.'

'My client's not the sort who forgets.'

'He hasn't got your temptations, has he?' She squirmed closer. 'Pity your client's not a woman. You're so good with women — you know that, don't you?' He went to the door, and she said: 'About

114

that money . . . if you're here next week, I'll let you have a little on account. And the rest in kind. Right?'

He drove down through Barnet to Wembley.

Norman had only one real terror in life. It was that in some appalling disaster the office walls might inexplicably crumble and he wouldn't be able to sit here any longer. There would be no Mrs. Barsham on the other side of the desk and no voices answering through the intercom, 'Yes, boss' and 'Great,' and 'Leave it to me.'

He liked to go out and tackle a job himself sometimes when it was big enough and rough enough, or when he wanted some woman to hate him and then crave for him. But it was good to get back.

Mrs. Barsham followed him to his desk, flipping over the pages of her pad. 'Two messages you'll want to — '

'Just a minute.' He settled into his chair. 'Get Michael, will you?'

She buzzed the extension. There was an alert yap in the receiver. Norman said: 'Michael, I want you to put someone on

Mrs. Haydock. She's got till Monday.'

'We've tried the kid-glove treatment?'

'I have.'

Mrs. Barsham was apparently re-reading and making minor corrections to some shorthand she had taken in his absence. But Mrs. Barsham never needed to make even the most infinitesimal correction to her shorthand. She was discreetly not listening, but hearing everything; and blandly approving. She knew Veronica and had had dinner with the Leggetts and arranged Christmas and birthday presents for Veronica so that Norman didn't have to worry; but she smiled an admiring smile when she recognised the nuances of Norman making a sexual bargain with a woman foolish enough to have the bills stacked against her, or, in due course, declaring the bargain void.

Michael said: 'Not getting results?'

'Not the results our client requires.'

Michael snorted. 'Leave it to me, boss.'

Maybe Mrs. Haydock would dig out his home address and phone Veronica. Some of them did. Once upon a time Veronica had flown off the handle and screamed at him when she got calls like that. Now she didn't even mention them, or at most would say, 'Another poor bag throwing up her heart on the phone today — getting the chop, I suppose?'

He gave Mrs. Barsham a curt nod to show that he was ready now for the messages.

She said: 'The director of Campus Press says he'd like you to go out there this afternoon if you can manage it. They're ready to discuss terms.'

'Fine.'

They beamed at each other. They got the same kick, a shared exhilaration, out of a deal pulled off or one about to be pulled off.

'Shall I say three-thirty?'

'Say just that.'

This could be a steady, long-term commitment. Regular bread-and-butter income. The Campus Press did a big mail order line in encyclopedias, educational part works and literary classics. Many of those who filled in their trial coupon and then received a free introductory volume and a membership form did not read the small print on the form, or failed to interpret it correctly. Out of all those who wrote in, the company estimated that between fifty and sixty a week would try to opt out again within the first couple of months. Half of these were knowledgeable enough to be not worth pursuing. The others could be leaned on. A barrage of polite reminders followed by polite demands for money followed by brusque final demands for money usually scared them into paying up. It was in the closing stages that the crunch came. Campus Press threatened to take defaulters to court. Twice it had done so, and won its case. But the judge had been highly critical of the methods employed. Comments from the bench and in the trade press did the firm's image no good.

What was needed was not the expense and publicity of a tedious court case, but the expertise of a well-organised debt collection agency.

It looked as though the director of Campus Press had made up his mind.

'Next, please!' said Norman, tilting back in his chair

'Mr. Cooke from the bank. He says the

representative he mentioned to you is in town today, and could meet you. Is there any chance of you dropping in at the bank before lunch?'

Intuitively she had lowered her voice, lamenting the change of mood that this item was bound to cause.

'Blast.' This was something he could have done without.

'Did he say they had . . . any news?'

'He said he'd prefer to see you privately, when you had a minute.'

They didn't mention Harold's name. She must by now know as much about the whole bloody stupid tangle as he did, but deferentially she asked nothing out of place and carefully avoided listening to some of his protracted telephone arguments on the subject. She hadn't even, he realised, said a word about the letters which she knew full well he and Arlene had received. What was in them, why hadn't they been handed over to the police, why was there no coroner's inquest?

She must have her own ideas, and they wouldn't be far from the mark. But unless he spread the whole thing out in front of

119

her and took her into his confidence, she wouldn't say a word.

It was crazy. He trusted her more than anyone he knew — more, even, than his sister — yet he sensed that to be utterly frank with her on this, to admit her as an equal and invite her to share the problem, would alter the whole balance of their relationship.

He didn't like balances altered, as Mrs. Haydock was going to discover before the weekend.

'Tell him I'll be there just before noon.'

Thankfully, he reached for the breakdown of Campus Press figures and methods that Mrs. Barsham had placed ready to refresh his memory.

* * *

Cooke said: 'I thought we might have a quiet word before our Mr. Squires joins us.'

'Hm.' Norman kept it non-committal until he could discover whether the quiet word was helpful or just as useless as all the others had so far been.

'I take it,' said the bank manager, 'that your advertisements have produced no results?'

'We've had three letters, from different parts of the country.'

'Of any value?'

'All from crackpots.'

'Are you intending to intensify the campaign, if one may put it that way?'

'No,' said Norman, 'we're not.'

'Ah.' For some reason Cooke seemed relieved.

Norman said: 'If my brother-in-law's still alive, which I don't believe he is, then he's unlikely to come trotting home just because of a small ad in the paper. Even if he sees it. If he did walk out for some half-baked reason, or because his reason had gone completely, it'd take more than that to bring him back.'

'A valid point, Mr. Leggett.'

'And if it's not Harold, but some vulture taking the pickings from a corpse, then he's not going to show up and say please sir it was me, now, is he?'

Norman's bluntness distressed Cooke, but he wagged his head to concede a

121

further basic truth.

'Inspector Brewer had a word with me the other day. An extremely discreet word,' he hastened to add, as Norman creaked menacingly forward in his chair. 'As he told you, he is not empowered to take any steps to trace Mr. Grant — '

'If it *is* Mr. Grant.'

'If it's Mr. Grant,' Cooke yielded. 'Because if it's Mr. Grant, there's no illegality. What the inspector suggested — and I'm sure he will have mentioned it to you — was that as you feel so strongly that the signature on those cheques could have been a forgery, you might interest a newspaper reporter in the story. The police need more to go on before they can act. A newspaper doesn't mind taking, as it were, a flyer. You'd get wider coverage. More people would notice it, including . . . well, whoever it is.'

Inspector Brewer had indeed phoned Norman on this subject. Norman barked out the same reply as he had given then: 'And 'whoever it is', as you put it, would dive for cover.'

'And assuming it's Mr. Grant, he could

make quite a fuss about someone concocting a story like that.'

'Concocting?' Norman echoed. 'Look, I've no intention of being a party to concocting anything. All I want is to find where and who — '

'Exactly, exactly,' said Cooke hurriedly. 'I can assure you the bank doesn't want melodramatic publicity of that nature. I'm so glad we see eye to eye on that. Head office wouldn't be at all pleased with me' — he risked a man-to-man smirk — 'if that matter of the cheques were splashed all over the front pages. We try not to draw attention to the fact that you can acquire that much money all in one day. Particularly if you — ah — happen to come into possession of someone else's card and cheque-book.'

'It's too easy,' Norman accused him. 'You make it too easy.'

'It won't be so easy after this coming summer. New regulations to check more than one encashment a day. Until then, we'd sooner play the possibilities down.'

The manager had made his point. Norman didn't really give a damn about the man or his bank or their trepidation about possible fiddles. If publicity would have helped, he'd have organised it. Paid for it, or wangled it. But he was convinced it would contribute nothing at this stage.

He said: 'Where's this fellow you want me to meet?'

Squires was a thin, raw-boned man with a stoop. His right shoulder was pitched a couple of inches forward as though at the ready for someone who might want to shake hands. He had fidgety eyes. Norman assessed him at once as a professional ferret: he employed one or two such in the Pledge and Distraint organisation, and admired them even when they gave him the creeps.

'Mr. Squires,' said Cooke, 'perhaps you'll summarise for Mr. Leggett exactly what you've found.'

Squires sat turned half away from Norman. His head cocked to one side, he might have been listening to a barely audible tape recorder.

He said: 'I had copies made of the two photographs of Mr. Grant with which I was supplied. The one taken from the Chamber of Commerce group picture didn't print up very well, and I gather the passport photograph wasn't a good likeness.'

'Ever see one that was?' Norman grunted.

'At least the fact that Mrs. Grant found the passport,' said Cooke keenly, 'shows that Mr. Grant was not planning to leave the country.'

Planning to leave the world, you nit, said Norman; but only to himself, over and over again.

'I consulted all branches at which these cheques were cashed that day,' Squires continued. 'I also obtained permission from the other banks involved to interview their staff.'

'And?'

'Most of them had no recollection whatsoever of the customer.'

'Hardly surprising,' said Cooke, 'in view of the number of transactions we all have to cope with every day.'

'They were dead unobservant,' said Norman. 'All right, let's take that as read.'

Squires' dispassionate enunciation did not waver. 'Of those who do have a faint recollection, only one is positive about the identity of the customer. The counter clerk in Harkside is sure it was Mr. Grant.'

'From those pictures? They could have been anybody.'

'That's what the others say. Two think it could have been Mr. Grant, but won't swear to it. One of them said he wouldn't trust himself to pick the man out on an identification parade. That's about the size of it.'

Norman said: 'And where the hell is he now?'

Squires edged round on the chair, apparently sizing Norman up by an unblinking study of his left lapel. 'Strictly speaking,' he said, 'my assignment was only to elicit what I could from bank employees, within the bank's own terms of reference. Since I was in the area, however, I filled in a few hours between trains checking on the car question. It wasn't too difficult, with the progression so clearly defined in the sequence of cheques. I found the car hire garage at my third attempt.'

'The police could have done all this. They ought to have done it right at the start.'

'The police,' Cooke interposed patiently, 'have been given no valid reason for suspecting any illegality. That is the whole point, Mr. Leggett. Apart from your own personal disquiet, none of us have any grounds to institute an official investigation — neither the police nor, really, ourselves.'

Norman groaned. 'But you have been checking — '

'For our own satisfaction.'

'The car was hired,' said Squires, 'in the name of Harold Grant. The manager doesn't remember his face or anything else about him. But when he made out the form he put down the number of his driving licence, and says he wouldn't have booked the vehicle to a Harold Grant if the name on the licence hadn't been Harold Grant.'

'That could have been stolen, along with all the other bits and pieces.'

'Mr. Leggett, did Mr. Grant always carry all those things with him? Most of us leave our cheque-book at home, or in the office — we tend to be careless with such things.'

'Not Harold.'

'But to have all of them — cheque-book, bank card, pen, driving licence . . . You know, I'm sure the police would confirm that nine out of ten people leave their driving licence at home — in another suit, or in a drawer, or attached to an application for something or other and filed away in mistake.'

'Not Harold.'

It was impossible for these other people to visualise the real Harold. Arlene had often said his tidiness drove her round the bend. He emptied his pockets every night, stacking his money on the bedside table and laying his watch at such-and-such an angle under the lamp. When he changed his suit, he methodically transferred every item from one jacket to its place in the other, from one trouser pocket to another.

Squires said: 'It really does look as though Mr. Grant was intending to walk out. In my experience, that's what that set of factors adds up to.'

Cooke nodded encouragement at him, as though at a favoured pupil.

Norman said: 'Well, we've got this far.

Is there any chance of your continuing where you've left off, Mr. Squires — at my expense, of course?'

Squires raised an eyebrow at Cooke, and shook his head gently.

'Mr. Squires is on the bank security staff,' said Cooke. 'I'm afraid he is not permitted to accept outside commissions.'

Squires said: 'If you'd like me to recommend a reliable private investigator — '

'I'll allocate one of my own, thanks.' Norman was ticking off names in his mind. The third was the best. 'I've got some pretty shrewd boys on the payroll,' he said. 'I'll take one off routine work, and get him started. You'd be prepared to let me have details of the car hire firm, where the car was returned and when, and so on?'

Squires opened his wallet and took out a folded sheet of paper. He handed it across. His writing was pale and spidery, but the information was laid out in a tight, concise column.

He said: 'You do understand, Mr. Leggett, that you have to tread carefully?

If our quarry is Mr. Grant, he is perfectly entitled to cash those cheques, even if he does appear to have done so in a bit of a rush. He is entitled to live where he chooses and spend his money as he chooses. Assuming, of course' — he glanced at Cooke — 'the account was not knowingly overdrawn.'

'It was just within the amount available. Another twenty pounds, and I should have had to call on your guarantee, Mr. Leggett.'

'If you find him,' said Squires, 'you really have no legal grounds for doing more than report his whereabouts to his next of kin. I assume that will be Mrs. Grant.'

'It is.'

'Mrs. Grant, I suppose, could take steps.'

'Steps?'

'Well, an application for restitution of conjugal rights, or a demand for maintenance — '

'Let's leave it, shall we?' Norman growled. 'Just let's find him. Then I'll decide who does what.'

'And you'll let us know if you find anything?' said Cooke.

'I'll let you know, all right,' Norman promised grimly.

'I'll have my man phone in every day, and I'll have his progress plotted on the biggest map I can find. And I'll let you know — up the ladder or down the snake, I'll let you know.'

★ ★ ★

Idling through the traffic a few hundred yards from the bank, he remembered the magazines, which Veronica littered about the house or accumulated higgledy-piggledy on the bathroom stool. The back of one of them carried a more recent Campus Press advertisement than those clipped to his file. He had meant to tear the page off and keep it.

He decided to make a circuit and call in at the house. It wasn't far out of his way.

Arlene's Renault stood on the drive by the door. He found when he went in that she was having lunch with Veronica.

Veronica's shadowed eyes looked as dark as though he had blackened both of them with his fists. She put her knife and fork down with an unnecessary clatter and said: 'You're not expecting to be fed, are you?'

'No.'

'You didn't tell me you'd be in for lunch.'

'I've told you, no. I've only just dropped in to collect something.'

'You see' — she turned piteously to Arlene — 'he just drops in to collect things. Never to see me.'

It wasn't worth an answer. It was bad enough night and morning: he didn't see why he should have to suffer the same scratchy irritations in the middle of the day.

He headed for the stairs. Through the open doorway Arlene called: 'Any news?'

'The bank's sleuth has established the trail of the car. I'm going to let Sandy take over from there.'

He found the advertisement he wanted and tore it away from the magazine. Then he went downstairs again, and looked in on the two women, meaning it to be for only a moment.

Veronica snapped at once: 'What's that you've got?'

'The back page of a magazine — an ad I wanted.'

'That's one of my magazines.'

'You weren't thinking of clipping the coupon, were you? Sending off for a sample volume of — '

'You'd no right.'

Arlene said: 'I thought we might drive into Aylesbury after lunch.'

'Tearing up my magazines without as much as a by-your-leave,' said Veronica. He wondered how many she'd had before Arlene got here. 'Snooping about among my things.'

'I've only been up there thirty seconds,' he said contemptuously. 'And what would I be snooping for?'

Bottles, he thought. And thought that was what Veronica was looking so defiant about.

Then Arlene said: 'What you said about the car — you think that trail's going to lead somewhere?'

'If I put a man full-time on it, the way the bloody police ought to be full-time on it, I don't care what they say . . . one man full-time, we might find something.'

'Not Harold, anyway,' said Veronica. She sagged, picked up her fork, began to dab at a mush of sprouting broccoli with it.

He wanted to be clear of the place, to have a quick lunch and then get to grips with Campus Press. But he found that he was rooted where he was.

He said: 'You haven't got a clue.'

'You used to think I had a clue. I was good enough when you wanted to get round Freddie Knight or Lew or any of that lot.'

'Yes,' he said. 'You were good enough for getting round the Freddies and the Lews. But I don't have to get round like that any more. And for anything else, you haven't got a clue.'

Arlene frowned in bewilderment. 'Norman, what — '

'About Harold, for instance,' he said.

'Dearest Harold,' said Veronica. 'I'm glad you haven't found him. I'm glad he's . . . undisturbed.'

Now he was positive. He said: 'You did get that letter.'

She shook her head. It wasn't so much a denial as a refusal to pursue that line of argument. She said:

'Harold loved me, you know.'

'Talk sense, will you?'

'He did. I'm sorry, Arlene. I don't want to hurt you, but he did love me. Really and truly. I'm sorry.'

'Don't apologise,' said Arlene sceptically.

'That's why he couldn't go on living. It all got too much for him.'

'Where's the letter?' said Norman. 'What did it say?'

'You're not going to ruin my memories of Harold,' said his wife.

He tossed the sheet of paper on to the coffee table and advanced on her. She uttered a high little gasp of a laugh. Arlene opened her mouth in an instinctive protest; then closed it again.

Norman said: 'Did Harold tell you in that letter precisely what he was going to do?'

'I don't want to talk about Harold. Not with you. Not the way you two talk about him.'

'Did he write to you or didn't he?' he shouted.

Her head jerked back as though he had slapped her face, but she glared back at him. He hadn't seen her so determined for a long time. It added to his assurance: she wouldn't have mustered this reserve of strength in defence of a figment of her imagination — or just for the hell of it.

Slowly, very slowly, he said: 'Oh, now, listen. He sent you a letter. All you have to do is show it to us. For all our sakes.'

'All our sakes?' The echo went sour in her mouth.

'How much did he say? Was there any mention of the firm? Of any of our dealings?'

'One of the lovely things about Harold was that we never said a word about business. You've no idea how wonderful it was. It was something you'd never understand, either of you.'

Arlene said in her mildest, friendliest tone: 'Veronica, I don't think you grasp quite how much we rely on you.'

Veronica tittered.

'If Harold did write to you,' said Arlene, 'I'm glad. For his sake and for yours. But if you've got an affectionate, purely personal letter telling you of his intentions, it really would be a help — to all of us — if we could show it to the police as proof — '

'No. Not the police. Not anybody.'

'So there *is* a letter,' Norman flared up.

'I didn't say so.'

He spun round and went for the stairs again. There was a clatter from within the room as Veronica knocked a plate aside and came after him.

'Don't you dare!' she was screaming. 'If you touch anything of mine . . . if you . . . '

He stormed into her room. She came sobbing in after him and grabbed him vainly by the arm. He shook her off.

She reeled against the dressing table, and he knocked her out of the way so that he could drag the drawers out and drop their contents on the floor.

She beat her fists about his head. He hardly felt her.

'The letter,' he said. 'Where is it?'

She tried to stop him opening the top right-hand drawer of the corner chest. When it came out, a half-empty bottle rolled across the floor.

'Looks as though it's time you went back for another cure,' he panted. 'A longer one, this time.'

'Norman, you wouldn't!'

'Where's that letter?'

'No,' she said, aimless yet utterly set in that negative. 'No, no.' She leaned against the white mantelpiece.

He opened the leather box of silver-backed brushes he had given her years before.

'It's no use,' she said.

He turned with his arm moving, ready to knock her sideways.

Near her bowed head was the clock Arlene had given them as a wedding present. He couldn't hang about here. Campus Press was important.

He tried to throttle his voice down. 'Veronica . . . '

'It's no use,' she said again.

'If we could produce that letter — a perfectly straight-forward, innocuous letter — telling the world he went out that night with the obvious intention of — '

'No.' It was hardly more than a sigh.

'Before I've finished,' he said, 'I'll beat the — '

'Yes, Norman. Yes, I'm sure you will. But you'll never find it.'

6

The sea had become a glistening pond, swaying with the viscous laziness of heavy-hued oil. A ship like a black splinter hung in mid-air, riding a feather of bleached cloud above the blurred horizon.

Two men in oilskins sat hunched on stools close to the water's edge. Their fishing rods were settled on tall tripods, and they watched the rock and swing of the sea with contentment rather than optimism. Some nights there would be gleaming lanterns all along the shore, and men between sixteen and sixty would sit by windbreaks or under huge umbrellas, one hand clutched round a pocket warmer, the other spasmodically pouring rum or hot coffee into a cup screwed into the shingle.

Judith kept to the extreme rim of the promenade as she approached the chalet where she'd had trouble with the three young strangers. But there was no sign of them. A new lock shone from the door, and the glass panes had been boarded over.

She reached the spot where sand was heaped up by the tide almost to the level of the concrete, powdery here but thickening as it broadened out towards the dunes. The converted smokehouse, its walls and chimneystack still coated with creosote, stuck up above the flimsier shacks and the two larger holiday houses.

A girl in a white sweater and pink skirt chased a dog along the shore, jumping from one erratic ridge of pebbles to another. The dog was jubilant, the girl absorbed in judging quickly where to put her feet. She slithered, jumped, and balanced for a split second on a tilting plank.

Judith trudged through the sand towards the smokehouse.

The girl tripped over a timber of breakwater nearly submerged in sand, picked herself up, laughed and glanced round, hoping no one was watching. Then she went on, the dog leaping and laughing about her.

One wall of the smokehouse had been extended to encompass a wooden shed, converted into a bedroom. A long, low window looked out to sea, its metal frame pitted with weed-green flecks.

Through the window, Pearson saw her coming.

He opened the door and was waiting for her as she clambered the hard-packed slope.

'Morning coffee?' he invited. 'Or a glass of sherry?'

'I mustn't stay. I've got someone coming for a lesson in half an hour.'

'A more promising pupil than me, I hope.'

She said: 'Would you mind awfully not having a lesson this afternoon?'

He was quizzically watching her mouth. His concentration was disconcerting: he seemed intent on extracting the last ounce of meaning out of everything he saw, heard and did — out of playing the piano, reading the notes on the stave, contemplating her face. Even staring out to sea, she thought absurdly, as though the sea might not be there for ever. Now he appeared to be more fascinated by the movement of her lips than by what she was saying. But he had heard all right. He said:

'Yes, I should mind awfully.'

'Oh. In that case we'll leave things as they are.' She was struck by the way, after such a short time here, he was crinkling his eyes in characteristic local fashion against the vast reflector of the sea. 'I'll tell her,' she said.

'Tell who?'

'One of the more difficult mothers. She's only just let me know that her precious Pamela's got a practice for some show jumping thing tomorrow. But she mustn't neglect her piano, so please may she have her lesson today.'

'Getting their money's worth?'

Money's worth, thought Judith dourly. Three bills covering lessons for the last six months had still not been paid. The Mallards didn't believe in settling bills. If you reminded them, they made it clear that you were unspeakably vulgar. Shopkeepers who complained lost their custom and the custom of their friends: the Mallards had ways of distributing hints that became social imperatives

'Actually,' she said, 'they're insufferable. I'm sorry I bothered to ask you.'

'But of course I don't mind swapping. I only meant that I would mind . . . not seeing you at the appointed time.' Before she could answer, or even decide what to answer, he said: 'Would you like me to meet Peter out of school tomorrow? Save you a bit of a scramble.'

'Oh, I can manage that. I always do.'

'I know. But take it easy for once. I'd love to collect him and have a stroll round.'

'Mr. Pearson — '

'Oughtn't it to be Harry by how? I'm sure you call your other pupils by their Christian names.'

'They're not quite the same.'

'A lot younger than me? Go on, say it.'

She said: 'I must go.'

'I'll walk you to the top of the cliff.'

'Honestly,' she said, 'if you'd sooner not postpone your lesson I don't see why you should have to. I wish I hadn't mentioned it.'

'I've got all the time in the world.'

'Until Easter.'

It had become a joke between them. When she said it the puckish little creases ran out from his eyes and nose and mouth. At first he had said the words with a troubled undertone that wasn't funny. Now it was a stock phrase. She was surprised just how many little throwaway phrases they tacitly shared after such a brief acquaintanceship. Even little flourishes on the piano keyboard, based sardonically on one of his most persistent fingering errors, had become a kind of private, personal communication.

They reached the lookout.

'So I'll meet Peter,' said Harry Pearson decisively, 'and wheel him home to you in good order. Or would he like to kick a ball about on the Common for half an hour?'

'It's pretty dark by the time he comes out.'

'Not all that dark.' They lingered by the churchyard wall, and with enough of a humorous tinge to cancel out a possible criticism he said: 'You'd sooner he didn't play about on the way home — get mixed up in any rough games?'

'I . . . oh, I suppose he ought to get out and about a lot more. He doesn't mix enough with the other boys. I know, I know. But I hate him to be out. I want to know he's home and safe and . . .' She shook her head, deriding her own fussiness.

'Afraid he'll fall in the sea?' Then he said, stricken: 'Oh God. Of all the dreadful things to say.'

'It's all right,' she said. 'It is, truly. A good thing to say it out loud every now and then, and face it.'

He put his hand on her arm. Again she was startled: startled by her immediate response to his touch.

Then he said: 'What the hell's going on?'

It was different. Not the same subject, the same emotion. She saw it a few seconds later than he had done, and was jolted by the same shock that had jolted the question out of him.

The row of shrubs along the church-yard path had been uprooted and tossed into a heap. Spades, picks and crowbars were stacked against the end of the Cruden monument, one slab of which

146

had been prised away from the side facing the path. Three strands of white tape stretched at intersecting angles between wooden pegs, thrumming white lines crossing some of the shallower grave surrounds and cutting between others.

'What are they doing?' Judith marvelled.

'Obviously not waiting for the sea to carry the bones away.'

They moved on a few paces; and in the lee of the church saw several headstones that had been taken up and propped like hefty playing cards against the wall.

'They can't be shifting the graves,' said Judith. 'Harry . . . they can't do that, can they?'

'John Cruden, Master Mariner.' he said softly. 'And good old Angus McMenemy.' And then, with a shaky laugh: 'Over my dead body!'

★ ★ ★

' . . . and regret the necessity of pointing out that, in keeping with our status as reputable credit referees available for consultation by major finance and merchant houses throughout the country, we shall feel it our duty to record your long overdue debt in any report commissioned from us unless recovery of this outstanding ten thousand pounds can be implemented by . . . '

The phone rang. Mrs. Barsham spun her pencil between right thumb and forefinger, and flicked the receiver up into her left hand. The faintly roseate nails curled around the lime-green plastic.

'Just one moment, please.' She held out the phone to Norman. 'It's George Sandy.'

'On the dot.'

'But of course,' she said admiringly.

The hard little voice, lilting central European plus twenty years of Birmingham adenoids, said: 'I'm on my way.'

'So's Apollo the umpteenth. When's splashdown?'

'The person calling himself Harold Grant' — Sandy was shrewd, nicely calculating how Norman would like to hear it expressed — 'left his hire car at a garage in Great Yarmouth.'

'Yarmouth? What on earth would he want there?'

'The firm in Coventry has a reciprocal

arrangement with six other places, four of them East Coast holiday resorts. Pick up your car at any one of them, sign it off at any one. Our friend signed off in Yarmouth.'

'That same day?'

'The following day.'

'Why didn't the bank's tame sleuth find that out?'

'I suppose he hadn't the time, and — '

'And strictly speaking,' Norman intoned derisively, 'it wasn't his job. All right, go on.'

'They wouldn't have been able to locate the car for him at that time without ringing round. A distribution chart is made up only at the end of each month, when they check who's got what and whether anyone has overstayed his hire agreement. Yarmouth had used this car a couple of times itself since its arrival, and it had only just been recorded on the Coventry chart when I got there.'

'Get over to Yarmouth, then.'

'That's where I am right now,' said Sandy complacently.

'Any joy?'

'The manager remembers the man vaguely, because he chatted a bit, asked a few questions, while he was waiting for the carbon of his booking chit to be worked out — you know, rebate or excess mileage, whichever way it went.'

'I know.' They had once done a gutting operation on just such a firm's books when establishing two large contract hire debts. 'What were these questions he asked?'

Sandy said: 'He wanted to know of a nice quiet little seaside place where he could have a few weeks' holiday.'

'Holiday? At this time of the year — and in that part of the world!'

'The manager thinks he remembers saying something about Cromer, and Wells, and Blakeney. And about the coast on the Suffolk side — Southwold, Dunwich, Ormeswich, Aldeburgh and so on.'

'And so on,' Norman echoed. 'Quite a range.'

'He didn't want to hang on to the car. So he'd have to go by train or coach. The trains don't get you far in these parts. The East Suffolk line heads inland from Lowestoft, and getting from any station on it to the coast needs a bus — and there aren't many of those, either. If he wanted to go north to Cromer or anything up there, he'd have to take the train in to Norwich for a start. No, I'd say he'd be more likely to use a coach if he wanted one of the quiet, remote places — which is what he was asking about.'

'You'd better start at the top, then, and work down.'

'First,' said Sandy, 'I'm checking the coastal express services leaving within an hour or two of when he signed off the car. If he stayed on in Yarmouth for a night or two, of course, I'm stumped.'

Norman said: 'Don't hang around. Get down to it.'

'I'll do that.'

'One thing . . . '

'Yes, Mr. Leggett?'

'Did the manager at the garage identify him? I mean, you did show him the photographs?'

'I did. He said they could have been him, or they could have been someone else.'

Norman was tired of hearing it. 'All

151

right. Contact me tomorrow.'

'I'll do that.'

Norman stared at the squiggles and cross-hatchings he had accumulated on the pad. To rob a corpse, hide it, grab as much money as possible . . . and then arrive in Yarmouth at the bleakest time of the year in search of a quiet holiday village for a few weeks — it didn't add up. The man must be mad.

If it was Harold . . .

But it wasn't. If there was one thing that just had to be so, it was that Harold was dead.

If it's Harold, he vowed, I'll flaming well kill him.

* * *

The rhythm of the *furiant* surged thunderously up from the bass. A pot on the brass table near the piano rattled a tinny resonance. Judith laughed, and carried the dancing figures of the treble impetuously up the keyboard, their rhythms crossing and clashing with Harry Pearson's sturdy three-four.

They raced to a conclusion. Judith laughed again.

'What did I do wrong?' asked Harry, breathless.

'Nothing. Nothing at all. Or if you did, I was enjoying myself too much to notice.'

They sat side by side, the music of the duet version of Dvorak's Slavonic Dances opened before them. The sonorities seemed to echo on inside the piano. There had been some funny moments, when the four-handed version didn't seem to work, and they were pushing one another from side to side, his right arm tangled with her left.

'I never thought I'd risk tackling anything like that,' he said.

'Another year,' she said, 'and I'd consider including you in my annual concert — just to show all the Mums what can be achieved for their little Tommies and Tessies.'

He studied the music for a moment, then pointed to a leaping phrase in the bass. 'We managed that rather well, I thought.'

'Rather well,' she agreed.

Still the echoes didn't die. She was

hearing music, and going on hearing it, as she hadn't done for some years now. Teaching Harry, she was learning from Harry: learning to listen again. Drudging through a succession of children each week, wincing over their scales, ploughing through the set pieces for the various grade examinations until she never wanted to hear them again in her life, she had forgotten what music itself was really about. Harry had reawakened old joys.

In his company, she realised with a shock, her whole life had acquired a keener flavour.

She got up hurriedly from the piano stool.

'Scared to try the next one?' he challenged.

'That'll have to be all for today. I've got to give Peter something to eat before he goes out.'

'I thought you didn't like him out after dark.'

'Playing rough games?' She still wanted to laugh, still felt the beat of the dance in her wrists and a muscle down her right calf. 'He goes to a chess club at his class master's home. It's only round the corner.'

Harry got up. 'My studio's free for my hour's private thumping in the morning?'

'Of course.'

He was reluctant to leave. She was reluctant to let him go, marking the beginning of another evening that might just as well not exist for all the differences it could display from any other evening. He stood where he was — medium height, casual in slacks and light cardigan, casual in the way he tended to lean his weight on his left leg rather than his right — not so casual when he said:

'If Peter's happily accounted for, would you come out and have a bite to eat somewhere? *The Galleon* or the *White Hart* — which do you recommend?'

She felt her cheeks burning. It was silly. The heater, and the speed at which they'd taken that dance, which was called a *furiant* but never intended to be so furious . . .

'That's awfully nice of you,' she said, 'but there's Major Kendrick.'

'Where's Major Kendrick?'

'I do him a meal every evening. We usually have it together — it's easier.'

'Let him have it on his own tonight. Leave the washing up, and come out with me.'

'No, I couldn't, really.' Without having planned it she heard herself say. 'Why don't you stay? Have it with us.'

'I asked if you'd come out with me.'

'Please. It'd be nice if you'd stay.'

'Making two portions stretch to three. No, that wouldn't be fair. Major whatsis-name wouldn't like that.'

'Please,' she said.

He stayed.

Major Kendrick was by nature too courteous to look put out when he found that a third party had been invited to dinner, but his quiet civility towards Harry somehow underlined the fact that she had made a momentous decision.

One eyebrow, bushy and white with a few lingering traces of grey, did rise involuntarily when Judith offered them both a glass of sherry. He had shyly given her the bottle for Christmas, mumbling and backing out of the room after its presentation, and had steadfastly refused to take as much as a glass with her. 'It's for you,' he had insisted. Now he watched as she poured a glass for Harry, and tried to wave away her invitation to one himself, but finally accepted, and smiled, and inhaled, and sipped. 'Ah,' he said. 'Yes. Hum. Well — cheers.'

Mercifully, she had put a stew in the oven. It was only a matter of peeling a few more potatoes, which she did while Peter ate baked beans on toast.

She saw him to the door, and kissed him, and stood on the step watching him lope down the street. He was getting so tall — taller than Jim had been, threatening to be a beanpole like her father.

Through the window she saw Harry's profile, and Major Kendrick's dome of a head with its thick ruff of hair behind the ears and down his neck. She would have to remind the major some time next week to go and have his hair cut. Trim and precise in everything else — polishing his shoes even though it hurt him to stoop, shaving, fastening the knot of his tie so that the diagonal stripe bisected it exactly the same every day — he never noticed when the tangle of his hair was growing too luxuriant.

The two men's heads bobbed awkwardly to and fro as they made spasmodic conversation.

A shadow drifted slowly along the opposite pavement. Its pale, unidentifiable face was turned towards the lighted window. Judith went back indoors and drew the curtains.

Two minutes after she had put the potatoes on to boil, there was a ring at the doorbell.

'Mrs. Marshall?'

'Yes.'

'I believe you let rooms.'

He stood on the lower step, a few inches below her. The hall light was yellow in the pallid creases of his face. He was not looking at her, but past her.

'Only one room, I'm afraid. And it's taken at the moment.'

'How long before it's vacant?'

'I've had Major Kendrick here for three years. No, getting on for four,' she said. 'I don't think he's in any hurry to move.'

'Major Kendrick?' The gashes of his features twisted into puzzlement. 'Not a Mr. Grant?'

'No.'

'Sorry,' he said. 'I must have got the wrong address. Or misunderstood what somebody said.'

But he was still trying to peer past her, as though summoning someone into the hall to confirm or deny what she had said.

'I'm sorry,' said Judith, and closed the door.

When they ate, Major Kendrick kept glancing at Harry Pearson. Then he would nod at his plate. Harry nodded back.

'Spoiled,' said the major suddenly.

'I beg your pardon?' said Judith in mock amazement.

'Spoiled,' the major said to Harry. He twinkled. 'I'm speaking of myself, of course — not the food. I'm spoiled. Fed like a fighting cock.'

'I can see that.'

After a while Kendrick said: 'Staying in the district long, Mr. Pearson?'

'Until Easter.'

Harry winked at Judith. It had become

a joke, like the tagline of some radio or television comedy show. Judith found it wasn't funny any more.

'Unusual time of year for a holiday. Or you're here on business?'

'More a period of . . . recuperation. Taking it easy while I think things out.'

'Re-mustering at Easter, eh?'

'At Easter.'

Judith watched as they made their tentative advances, edging on from polite platitudes to cautious exploration of each other's interests.

Major Kendrick asked: 'Play snooker?'

'I used to. When I was . . . ' Harry stopped, then said: 'Not for years.'

'I try to keep in trim. The odd afternoon, every now and then. Passes the time until we all stop breathing.'

'Really, Major!' Judith protested.

'Oh, it's all right, my dear. I know what some folk in the town call the Club — God's waiting room.'

'I'm sure I've never heard it called that.'

'You don't listen to those sort of people,' said Kendrick affectionately. He forked up his last cube of meat and ate it with relish, then dabbed a smear of gravy from his chin and impishly sucked his finger. To Harry he said: 'We really do pile up some records, you know. Ormeswich . . . well, you survive the first six months here and you'll live for ever.'

'I pointed out Mrs. Ainsworth to Mr. Pearson a week or two ago,' said Judith.

'Absolutely. There you are, you see.' Kendrick beamed with the pink, placid boastfulness of those who choose to live perpetually exposed to wind and cold, ten miles from a main road, on a crumbling coastline in constant peril of inundation by the sea, fifteen miles from the nearest railway station — 'And that,' said Major Kendrick gleefully, in the best British backs-to-the-wall tradition, 'is scheduled for closure, when they've got the guts to go through with it.'

He went on to tell their guest about the Flower Arranging Society, the Marsh Bird Preservation Society, the Godyll Club of which he was a member, the Saxon Shore Preservation Society . . .

'And speaking of preservation,' Harry smoothly interrupted, 'what about the churchyard? Just what *is* going on there?'

Judith and the major began to speak at once. He deferred, said, 'I'm so sorry, my dear,' and waved her on. But she said: 'No, Major, you've talked to a lot more people than I have.'

Kendrick said: 'It's a disgrace. Sheer laziness. Vicar handed over upkeep of the churchyard to the town council twenty years ago. Didn't know you could do that. Anyway, they've been responsible for mowing it and keeping it tidy. Now they say it's too much trouble — takes too long to clip the grass, clip the edges, that sort of thing. So they're going to tear up all the gravestones, and the trees — '

'The double cherry,' Judith lamented. 'The flowering shrubs.'

'Just so they can get a clear run for a motor mower?' said Harry.

'That's about it, old chap.'

Harry said: 'Have they got a Faculty?'

'None of them in working order, if you ask me,' grunted Kendrick.

'No, I mean a Faculty for . . .'

Judith gathered up the plates, went out, and returned with a lemon soufflé. The major, momentarily distracted from the conversation, chortled. 'Now don't tell me,' he said archly. 'It's got to last two nights — yes?'

'Yes.'

'And the Dilapidations Commission,' Harry was urging.

'Are you sure the council have gone through the right procedure? Because if not, they can be stopped in their tracks.'

'The vicar says he's on their side,' said Judith. 'Or so I've heard.'

'Ought to be ashamed of himself,' said Kendrick.

'You really ought to make sure they know what they're doing, before they go too far and ruin the place.'

'Hum,' said Kendrick. His attention veered towards the soufflé. 'Delicious,' he said after a mouthful. He glanced at his watch, muttered something to himself, dropped it back into his waistcoat pocket, and began to eat more quickly.

When they had finished and were getting up, he said: 'You will excuse me, won't you? Must go and get spruced up. Don't want to lower the Club standards, you know.' He chuckled. The presence of a newcomer at table had livened him up. 'Tell you what,' he said at the door. 'You must come and have a game one day. Come as my guest.' Then, looking rather shaken by his own impetuosity, he beamed and vanished.

Ten minutes later they heard him coming downstairs and opening and softly closing the front door.

'I'll give you a hand with the dishes,' said Harry.

'You'll do no such thing.'

She moved away from the table. He cut across her path. 'When I say I'll give you a hand . . . ' His hand was on her forearm, and wouldn't go away.

'Please,' she said meaninglessly.

He was looking at her lips again.

He said: 'Judith.'

She had never before heard her own name sound like music.

His arm was round her. She was pulled hard against him. 'No,' she sobbed. But that, too, was meaningless. Every nerve and muscle in her body cried something that denied it.

She was hungry — hungrier than she had ever admitted in all these years of abstinence. Not with some wild greed, to be satisfied by anyone who came along. But hunger, there all the time, gnawing at her, waiting.

And now there was Harry.

He stopped looking at her mouth and tasted it. Her fingers and his fingers played a different kind of duet now — gentle then fierce, legato and then savagely staccato.

'Damn you,' she cried in a loving crescendo.

His hands tortured her into ecstasy. They were too strong, too frightening. The hands of the man who had savaged those three youngsters on the promenade.

Gentle cruel hands.

'No.' Her head was twisted back against the couch, her lips close to his ear, sobbing again.

'Yes,' he said hoarsely. And at last, drawn out of him on one long, shuddering breath: 'Judith . . . '

When they were still, the ordinariness of the room and the world around them came seeping back into her consciousness. The light ached in her eyes. She hadn't finished clearing the table. A clock ticked faintly. But there was no clock in the room: she wouldn't have a loudly ticking clock here — it was difficult enough as it was to keep some of the kids on the right beat.

It was Harry's wristwatch, whispering its steady tempo against her cheek.

She sat up, pushed her hair back and looked into his sated eyes. In this drowsy aftermath she couldn't believe in violence — not even the brief, shattering violence of a few minutes ago. She wanted to stay here, hot and crumpled and happy, for ever.

She said: 'Peter'll be home very soon.'

He kissed her once more, said 'Judith' once more — this time tenderly and reflectively — and they got up.

It was not until they were at the front door that she remembered opening the door to the stranger, just before dinner, and without thinking she said:

'Do you know anyone called Grant?'

He made no perceptible movement;

166

but she was still part of him, still in tune with him, and she knew that he had stiffened.

'What makes you ask that?'

'Somebody was here, at the door. Just before we sat down to eat. Asking about rooms, and whether I'd got a Mr. Grant here.'

'Asking . . . here?'

They had been so warm, and now she was so cold. 'Do you know a Mr. Grant?' she said.

'I did. Once.'

Just before she closed the door behind him he turned and caught her hand, clutching it painfully between those tough, wiry fingers. He smiled a taut smile, and was gone.

Judith went back in, and drew aside one of the curtains a few inches. It was pathetic, at her age; but she wanted to watch him walk away and turn the corner.

He reached the corner and disappeared without looking back.

As she let the curtain slide between her fingers, she had a fleeting impression of a shadow detaching itself from the darkness of a privet hedge opposite and heading for the same corner. By the time she had tugged the curtain open again, there was no sign of anyone in the street.

★ ★ ★

'Whoever he is,' said Sandy along a twittering line, with two women's voices arguing interminably behind him, 'he calls himself Pearson.'

'You're sure it's him?'

'No, I'm not sure. Not absolutely sure. But he's the likeliest one yet.'

'If this is another false alarm — '

'Boss, short of marching right up to him and asking him outright who the hell he is, I can't be sure. And even then he could just look me in the eye and say he doesn't know what I'm talking about — and flit off again at the first opportunity.'

'He's not to flit off,' snarled Norman. 'Keep an eye on him until . . . '

'Until when?'

The chirrupings on the line grew worse. Norman said: 'Where can I ring

168

you this evening?'

'I'm staying in a crummy guesthouse.'

'So I should hope. I'm not paying winter cruise expenses.'

'That's what I thought.' Sandy dictated the number. Norman scribbled it down, and said:

'Seven sharp this evening. And I'll want the address and every single little detail you've got.'

'I don't have all that much yet.'

'Then go out and grab some more. I mean evidence, not guesswork.'

By seven he had summoned Arlene to the house and installed her beside the bedroom phone extension. He prepared to make the call downstairs. Veronica said: 'Can't I . . . ?'

He said: 'No, you can't.' She stared, transfixed, as he dialled.

Sandy reported: 'He's rented a shack on the beach. Until Easter. Paid cash — the whole lot in advance. He seems to know quite a few people, but one of the grocers says he's not a local. Just muscled in. Two days ago he got mixed up in some group that's trying to stop the council digging up a graveyard.'

'A graveyard?'

'Seems there's one lot want to shift the stones out of the churchyard and another lot want them kept there.'

'Are you following the right trail? Why should a grave-robber . . . only there wasn't any grave, but all the same if he's the one who stole from the body . . . look, why should he want to get involved with gravestones in . . . '

In Norman's chest was the burning sensation he always suffered when someone tried to take him for a ride.

Sandy said: 'And he's taking regular piano lessons.'

'What kind of monkey are you making out of me?'

'Boss, I've checked him out as far as I can. There's something phoney about him. And it could all fit: the date he arrived, the way he spends cash, the description — he could be that Mr. Grant in the picture.'

'Or he could be someone quite different.'

'I never got to see your Mr. Grant when he was in the firm. But Mr. Leggett, the dates, the cash . . . living on his own . . . except he's got this thing going with this piano teacher, according to the grocer on the corner.'

The added resonance on the line might have been Arlene taking a sharp intake of breath, or just Sandy shifting the mouth-piece in his hand.

Norman said: 'Right, then. Tell me the rest. His address. Where he's likely to be and when. Does he suspect you're on to him? Does he . . . '

Sandy rattled off the details. In the middle of them, Arlene spoke. 'Does he have a limp?'

'Who was that?' Sandy gasped.

'Never mind. Answer it.'

'A limp? Not that I've noticed. But hold it a minute. You could say he favoured his left leg a bit. Not what you'd call a limp: just a sort of way of walking.'

When they had finished, Arlene came downstairs.

'He's nuts,' said Norman. 'He's picked another dud.'

Veronica said: 'Who is it?'

'Nothing to do with you.' Norman

stumped about the room. 'All that stuff about the piano. Why should some cheap lifter want to — '

'Harold used to play the piano,' said Veronica with dreamy irrelevance.

'First I've heard of it.' Norman looked inquiringly at his sister.

Arlene said: 'He used to. Just messing about. He was never any good; said so himself.'

'But he wanted to be.' Veronica's dreaminess erupted into ferocity. 'He always wanted to play better. Said if he'd had the time, and things had been different . . . '

'What things?' Arlene demanded.

'If you have to ask, it shows how insensitive you were.'

Norman said: 'Cut that out.'

'He played for me a couple of times. When you weren't around. He had a wonderful touch.'

'And you were touched?' Norman made a dirty word of it.

Veronica circled him and made for the door. 'If you've finished with my room, I'll go up and lie down.'

They let her go.

Arlene said: 'Did you ever find that letter?'

'No. It's there all right, somewhere. But a sheet of paper's easier to hide than a gin bottle.'

'Writing to Veronica,' she mused, incredulous. 'And all this about a piano teacher.'

'It's not Harold. Not both things, not like that.'

'Isn't it?'

'It doesn't fit.'

'I'd like to see that letter. More than anything I'd like to see that letter.'

He said: 'You know what Ron is, don't you? She's a very special kind of nympho.'

'If you're telling me that she and Harold — '

'Nothing like that. It's all a matter of . . . look, she's always had to have someone fussing around her. Big production number, all the time. She got a crush on anyone, anyone at all, who made her feel important.'

'All those drunken yobs you used to knock about with?'

'All she wanted was to have them put on the act. Paw her, put their arms round her, breathe all over her. Smooching, making a meal of it.' Norman wiped his neck with his right palm as though to rub away some stickiness. 'It never went further than that. But there always had to be someone around making out he'd love to have her if he could get her.'

'Not so many of them around just lately.'

'No.'

'So you think she fixed her sights on Harold — and Harold wrote her that kind of letter?'

'If he didn't,' said Norman, 'she could talk herself into believing it was that kind of letter.' He looked up at the ceiling, conjuring up a picture of Veronica drifting about, opening a drawer, lying on her bed reading a scrap of paper. He restrained himself from trampling upstairs as fast as he could go. 'Sooner or later I'll beat it out of her. So help me I will.'

'First things first,' said Arlene with infuriating condescension. 'Now we've got a lead on this joker, we have to see

174

him. And decide.'

'I'll go down and take a look.'

'No,' she said. 'I'm the one to go.'

'Like hell you are.'

'I have to know. I have to find out what he's playing at.'

'You think it's Harold. You really do think it's Harold.'

'I've got to know. If it is him, then you can leave it to me.'

He couldn't credit it. 'You're starting to fancy him! And you used to tell me you couldn't even bear him to . . . ' He wiped the back of his neck again. 'How kinky can you get?'

'I never thought he was capable of — '

'He wasn't! He isn't! This,' he said slowly and heavily, 'is not Harold.'

'In which case, we have him hauled in and find out what did happen to Harold. And then the executors call all the money in. Including the house payment from you. And I get the insurance. And his holdings in the company were transferred to me before you set up the bankruptcy.'

'You'll be nice and comfortable. But remember who fixed it all.'

'If you want to go on fixing things,' she said, 'You'll have to do things my way. It's all in my name.'

'Don't you come the bossy bitch with me,' said Norman.

Their nerves were raw. They confronted each other, and he saw that she was his sister all right, and a whole lot tougher than he had reckoned. She would never be as easy as Harold had been. Whichever way the future worked out, the forecast was trouble.

Fine when she was on his side. Murder if she wasn't.

He said placatingly: 'One of us has to go. All right. It makes no difference. So long as you don't scare him off before we've found everything we have to know. So when you get there — '

'Yes,' she said. 'Yes, I know, I know. I'll report in every hour on the hour. Or at any rate,' she said, 'let's say tomorrow evening, when I'm good and ready, and when I've had time to find out exactly what it's all about.'

*　*　*

Arlene Grant set out at ten o'clock on the Wednesday morning and arrived at Ormeswich ten minutes before last orders for lunch were being taken in the White Hart. She had lunch, left her car in the hotel yard, and went out. Early in the evening she booked in for one night's bed and breakfast, made a telephone call, and dined alone.

A few minutes after six o'clock the following afternoon she was discovered at the foot of the cliff below the church. Two young men and a girl who had been scuffling along the beach from the south, intending to break into one of the deserted shacks in the dunes and squat and smoke there for a few days and nights until they were observed and thrown out, stumbled over the huddled shape. The girl screamed and ran off. The young men made as good an inspection as was possible in the pale glow of the evening sky. It was enough to make one of them lurch away and vomit. The other went after the girl and calmed her down.

They talked of getting out of the town quick. This wasn't the sort of mess they wanted to get mixed up in. But someone who had heard the girl's scream was peering over the railing of the lookout and shouting down at them. To run now was to invite worse trouble. Safer to report what they'd seen.

Brighter lights, including the police photographer's flash, showed the woman lying with her face driven hard into the sand and shingle. They also showed a wide cleft across the top of her head, and hair matted into a dark ooze of congealing blood.

7

Harold Grant realised he had made a mistake. He ought to have pulled the trigger that Thursday night. It would have been so simple. He had meant it to be simple and final. But he had made a mistake, and now all these complications had inevitably followed.

The revolver had been in his hand. It was cold but soothing against his right temple. He knew exactly how the bullet would enter and how immediate the end would be.

The footsteps along the lane came closer.

Right. Now.

A girl squeaked, a man said something; she giggled.

There were two lots of footsteps, lurching and stumbling over the dried mud.

It wasn't a pretty sight, a man with his head blown open.

Not for a girl. Not for a courting couple.

Harold lowered the gun.

Let them go past, and then he'd do it.

They didn't go past. They slowed, and muttered, and the girl giggled again. There was a splutter and crackle of twigs. 'It'll be so cold, it's prickly, it's . . . ' The man muttered, she shrieked with delight.

Not fair to blow your brains out quite so close to them.

Harold got to his feet. Quietly he walked away, along the towpath. Each time he stopped to choose another place he decided it wasn't far enough, and resumed his progress.

When at last he sat down, on the stump of a tree jutting out over the water, he felt cold and cramped.

He shifted his position. Something shoved into his hip. It wasn't the gun — he was still carrying that, clinging to it.

There was a bulk of something in one of his pockets. He realised that he was still carrying his new cheque-book. At the same time as he collected it, he had taken out thirty pounds in cash on the last cheque in his old book.

He rested the gun on his knee.

Some nocturnal creature flopped into the water a few inches below him, and in the hazed light he saw a slowly spreading wake expand across the surface.

He didn't have to finish right away. There was money in his wallet, and more potential money in his pocket. Somehow it struck him as tidier to get rid of it all before casting the ultimate balance. Strip himself of those tempting assets, and then draw a neat double line.

And why not? It wasn't that he was going to weaken; not going back to Arlene, or that disgusting office and disgusting job, to see Norman's face and hear his voice again or to see and hear the whining victims. Never that. But why not a month or two of relaxation, wherever he felt like going, just for the hell of it?

No coming back drearily from holiday, as he'd had to do when he was a child: when this holiday ended, it would end cleanly.

Stupid that it hadn't occurred to him before.

He felt light-headed as he scrambled back from the tree stump and went on along the path. A sparse straggle of lights marked a road climbing to a hump-backed bridge ahead. When he reached the bridge he leaned on the stile and wondered what road this could be. In all the years they had lived in that hideous house he had never walked this far in this direction. He hadn't even known there were narrow hump-backed bridges like this still in existence.

A car slid soundlessly downhill from one side and thumped across the hummock. Another changed gear on the slight incline to his right.

Sprawling down there was a lentil soup of sodium lighting. He would find a taxi . . . No, not a taxi. A bus would be safer.

He found the bus, found a train, spent the night in a Bayswater hotel chosen at random, and on Friday morning took a train from Paddington to Ruabon. Once there had been a branch line along the valley. It was there no longer. He took a bus to the village.

A mistake.

The whalebacked Welsh hills were the same. He could even, he was sure, have identified certain clumps of trees spreading their defiant arms against the rain-choked skies. But the valley was not the benevolent valley he remembered. His aunt had died a long time ago, and when he came to look back he found he'd had few close friends in the village. A few weeks a year — how could he have made lasting friends, who would remember him out of all the other visiting relatives and holiday-makers? There had been an ambience of friendship, that was all. None of it remained.

There were too many cars. The little sweetshop he remembered was now a tarted-up teashop with a painting of a demure Welsh maiden in a tall Welsh hat above the door. His aunt's house had been demolished to make way for a row of new houses, clean and not unattractive in their stylised alternation of Ffestiniog slate and Ruabon brick. But the poky back garden and its decrepit summer-house were obliterated. The path by the river began with a car park and petered out now in a bare patch impregnated with ice-cream and chocolate papers trodden in last summer.

Only one spot remained evocative. Several jagged slabs of rock thrust out into the river, submerged when it was in flood, humped above the surface like hippopotami when the level fell. He had spent hours out there, in the past, in the sunshine, not so much planning the future as wondering about it and wondering how good it was going to be. He stepped out there now, and sat there for five self-conscious minutes in the cold. The view had changed little: the bridge concealed the new service station on the far bank, and the plastics factory was behind him. The trees were spiky and leafless, but still where they ought to be.

But it had been summer then. Now it was winter.

He stayed a week, walking over the hills towards the more threatening mountains, or sitting in the lounge reading a succession of paperbacks from the news-agent's where he had once bought a boy's magazine and some sixpenny detective stories his aunt had disapproved of but never actually banned.

One year there had been a succession of nights in which planes had droned overhead on their way to bomb Liverpool. He had been sure that when he grew up he would stop them doing things like that.

From the same shop, this week, he bought several newspapers each day. He wondered whether Norman and Arlene, baffled by his total disappearance after sending them such explicit letters, would insert exploratory appeals in the small ads columns. If they had done so, he found none. Perhaps they couldn't make up their minds what was best at this stage.

He had to fight off the urge to phone Arlene or send a telegram saying she wasn't to worry, the stay of execution was only temporary, she wouldn't have long to wait.

And Veronica. He prickled with embarrassment about the futile letter he had written to poor Veronica. If he let himself think about that, he wouldn't enjoy his remaining weeks.

Think of something else.

'Play that again.' It was his aunt's voice. 'More slowly this time. Think about what you're doing, Harry. Think before you start.'

What had happened to his aunt's piano when she died, when the place was broken up, when he was in Korea? He had played it by the hour and she had sat in the same room listening, hearing him right through even when he was at his worst.

'You keep at it.' He hadn't heard that voice for years and would never hear it again, yet would never cease to hear it.

'There's no use it is dabbing at it off and on, like. You just keep at it, and what's there will be there.'

It had all been so important then; all part of one of those promises, the promises that slid away when you weren't looking.

His money was running low. There had been the new pyjamas, shaving gear, and a small suitcase. Fares, the hotel, food, drinks, papers and paperbacks and magazines ate up what was left. He ought to buy a couple of shirts and a pair of slacks, and a pullover or cardigan.

He was on the verge of making out one of the cheques in his new book when he realised that it was no good doing one at a time. That way they would soon be on to him: the banks must have some way of circulating branches when a supposedly dead man's signature began to turn up.

Supposing, of course, he was supposed to be dead.

He wished he could listen to whatever was going through Norman's and Arlene's minds.

He took a bus, and a train, and changed, and got to Coventry. There he hired a car, cashed all his cheques in one day, and knew that wherever he went from now on it couldn't be back into Wales. It had to be somewhere that meant nothing to him, or to anyone he knew and was likely to bump into.

Ormeswich chose itself. If a coach had been leaving Yarmouth for Mundesley or Sheringham ten minutes before the Ormeswich coach, it could just as easily have been Mundesley or Sheringham. As long as it was on the sea.

Suddenly that had become imperative. Not a Welsh valley, shut in below its scowling hills, crushing all memories, but somewhere cold and stark — and facing east, not west.

So it was Ormeswich.

He could have driven there. Could have explored the coastline, perhaps even found somewhere more picturesque. But he didn't want the car. He was in no mood for continuing travel. He wanted to settle and let what time was left drift over him, not to use it up. Besides, car hire was expensive. Money saved on that would subsidise a few more days of life.

Which was another mistake.

Those first few days in the old smoke-house he was carefree as he had never been in his life before. Half the trouble of living was the grinding obligation to plan for the future, worry about next year and the year after that — and about tomorrow. Investing in and for your children. Earning to save to invest to preserve so many things after you were too tired to know what the things were worth in themselves; tired, or dead.

Impossible to live in the present when you were fretting about the future. Only when you knew there would soon be a definable end to it all, and no further problems, could you taste the immediacy of life.

He met Judith Marshall.

The stumbling run across the sand and shingle had been instinctive. Old intuitions, jabbed into wakefulness, had recognised the mood of the group around the woman: the threat in that hunched boredom, to be released only in purposeless bullying. Automatically he was into the middle of them, punching and chopping. They didn't know what had hit them. They were on the receiving end of his own pent-up store of anger.

It was alarming how readily, almost gleefully, the old savage skills not only came back but took complete possession.

'You like it cold and lonely?'

They were walking towards the end of the promenade, he and the bright-cheeked woman with a strand of fair hair straggling from under her hood.

'I can do with a spell of that.'

That's what he had told her. It had been true. When he found it was ceasing to be true, it was too late.

Too late. The words no longer had their comforting ring.

There was Judith. There was the whole sharp, sparkling ambience of the town. There was young Peter. Wrong that he should so immediately find Peter better company than his own children — Arlene's children — had ever been. The whole situation was wrong.

Pathetic, to apply himself at last to practising the piano as he ought to have practised it thirty and more years ago.

Wrong to waste time, Judith's as well as well his own, learning and then snuffing out what he had learnt.

Arlene had made it impossible for him to persevere, or even to dabble. Just by being there she made it impossible.

He had lacked the incentive to make an issue of it — and, as time went by, also lacked the time.

Now that there was so little time left, there was all the time in the world.

Judith . . .

He tried to establish whether Harry Pearson was a different person from Harold Grant. In the past he had never succeeded in being anyone but Harold. Norman had boomingly called him Hal at one stage, but it hadn't worked. Some of Arlene's friends, trying to make themselves friendlier than they were entitled to be, had called him Harry and spoken about him as Harry to Arlene. She had looked puzzled.

Now he was Harry, waiting in a shop at Judith's elbow.

A tall woman in heathery tweeds stood ahead of them. She commanded the undivided attention of both the grocer and his daughter. A long, much corrected bill lay on the counter.

'Absolutely not. I did not have any delivery of any tinned puddings or of tinned apricots in Christmas week.'

The girl said: 'But I made a note — '

'Absolutely not.'

The girl looked at her father. He smiled apologetically, crossed the item out, and totted up another revised total.

'Oh, and I almost forgot. I didn't

mention it, did I? Three of that last lot of eggs I had from you were bad.'

Another line was scored through. Harry Pearson read the figures upside-down, calculating in his head faster than the grocer could manage. Or was this a flickering shade of Harold Grant?

'We've got some nice cheese in, only this morning, Lady Mallard.'

'Hm.'

Lady Mallard let her gaze range sceptically along the shelf. Then she picked up the bill, looked even more mistrustfully at it, folded it, and tucked it into her raffia shopping bag.

At the end of a long black lead she had a white poodle. Before she could turn to go it lifted one leg against a stack of sugar packets, and urinated vigorously.

They went out.

Harry said: 'Wouldn't buy that — too much urine in the sugar nowadays.'

The grocer smiled feebly, and hurried to ask Judith what she wanted. As they left, he called out, 'Good afternoon, Mrs. Marshall . . . Mr. Pearson.'

So he was Harry Pearson; and on the

way to acceptance.

'Don't they operate food shop laws here?' Now he knew he was Harold. 'I mean, that little dog — '

'Any shop in this town that bans dogs,' said Judith, 'will also ban its customers. They just wouldn't come in. Word would soon get round, and the place'd be out of business.'

'But surely if they all got together — '

Judith laughed.

Still succumbing to the encroachments of Harold, he said: 'I noticed that bill, by the time he'd finished with it. Quite apart from letting her bludgeon him into crossing off things he knew darned well she'd had, he gave her five per cent discount.'

'For prompt payment.'

'How prompt?'

'Whenever she's gracious enough to make it.'

'And you?'

'What about me?'

'What discount do you get?'

'I'm not one of those who run up an account there. He wouldn't refuse me, but he'd be embarrassed about it. I pay cash.'

'But if you pay cash, you ought to be allowed a bigger discount. Do you get it?'

'I don't belong, really,' said Judith. 'I come from the fourpenny end of the town.'

'You need a new deal here. A different sort of protection racket — not the usual sort.'

The sun silvered touches of frost on rooftops only now getting a breath of its pallid warmth. Afternoon shadows were spindly and distorted.

He took Judith's arm. It was soft and yielding.

He said: 'You don't ever feel like leaving — turning your back on a place like this?'

'I thought you liked Ormeswich.'

'I do. It suits me, right now. But I'd have thought for you, and for Peter . . . '

'I've got the house. I'm a . . . well, a part of Ormeswich. I was born here.'

'So were lots of others. Not many of the young folk stay, do they?'

'Not nowadays. There's nothing for them to do.'

'But you?' he insisted.

'I can't think of anything else.'

'You don't feel shut in?'

They reached a corner, and down the gentle slope to their right was a glimpse of railings and the grey glimmer of the sea beyond. Judith waved towards it. 'Shut in?' she laughed. Even when they walked on and a row of houses cut off the view, they could still hear the sea, as you could hear it everywhere in Ormeswich — its steady hoarse breathing, throbbing in alleys and whistling one special, individual high note at the corner of Ship Street.

'I did try going away for a while,' Judith said, 'after Jim died. There was a job in Maidenhead, a mixture of matron and music teacher at a private school. But it wasn't right. And I couldn't breathe there. Peter wouldn't have liked it. We were glad to get back.'

'Good old Angus.'

'Sorry . . . ?'

'My old chum, Angus McMenemy,' he said.

'Oh. Of course. The churchyard.'

'Couldn't tear himself away once he'd

settled here,' said Harry, 'until he got orders from head office.'

* * *

The Godyll Club was reached through a Georgian doorway cramped between a fishing tackle shop and a tobacconist's. Inside there was a steep flight of stairs, installed early in this century, smelling of damp and linoleum. At the top was a cramped hall, lit by a skylight, with three doors opening from it into the rooms of the Club.

The room into which Major Kendrick led Harry Pearson was about thirty feet square. It held two tables, only one of which was lit.

Kendrick squinted at two shapes beyond the table, their faces shielded by the canopy.

'I've brought Mr. Pearson in for a game.'

One man, tall and lanky, with closely cropped grey hair, shaggy tie and shirt and shaggy jacket, emerged, his lean face sliced into halves of light and shade.

'Mr. Pearson,' he said, holding out his hand.

'Our President,' said Major Kendrick, 'John Tucker. And when we can winkle him out' — his tone changed to one of clumsy adolescent banter — 'that'll be Pat Sherwill. Ex Royal Marines. It's all that slow marching — he's always late showing up.' A stocky, almost bald man stumped forward. 'Ah, got him into the open at last.' With an onset of shyness, as though still not sure if he'd got the pronunciation quite right, Kendrick said: 'And this is Pearson — Harry Pearson.'

'You're planning to take us on?' said Sherwill.

'If you'll bear with me,' said Harry.

'Handicap?'

'I haven't played for years. Must be twenty years.'

Not since the Army days — the waiting days, between training, when they weren't sure where to send you or what to do with you; the inevitable interminable days before things got rough.

'Oh yes?' said the President amiably. 'We've had your kind in before. Still, we'll take a chance and play you level. Fair enough?'

'Very fair.' Kendrick's shining eyes invited Harry to enjoy their company, and please to enjoy the privilege of being invited here.

Tucker said: 'We play for sweepstake tickets. Tenpence a head, and there's fivepence cue money. All right?'

'Fine,' said Harry.

Kendrick had lovingly taken his own cue out of its case and now, with Sherwill's help, set up the balls. While they were doing it, Harry selected a cue from the score or more in racks round the room. Most of them were lightweight, probably relics from the days of billiards' popularity, but he found one of seventeen ounces. He rolled it on the baize; it was reasonably true.

Sherwill was completing the table setting.

Harry edged past him. 'What are those?'

There was an orange-coloured ball on a spot midway between the blue and the pink, and a purple one midway between blue and brown.

'Snooker extra balls.' Sherwill had a low but imperious voice that retained the softest suspicion of a west-country inflection.

'Don't you know them?' When Harry shook his head, he explained: 'Orange counts eight and purple ten.'

The major, hospitably clarifying, said: 'We only use them when the Club is fairly quiet. They make the frame a bit longer. Flatter our game, of course. Get those two and you've got a twenty break with four balls.'

They tossed for break. Tucker won. He put the others in.

Kendrick broke off the right-hand side of the triangle, the cue ball coming back into baulk behind the green. Tucker said:

'You follow him, Pat. You like the easy ones.'

'Har bloody har,' said Sherwill, mellowly vindictive. 'I'm damn near snookered.'

He could see half of one ball at the far end. He brought the white back off it, almost to its original position: a good defensive shot.

A couple of reds were showing, but nothing any good. The others watched as Harry got his head down for the shot.

'I knew it,' said Tucker. 'Twenty years, the man says — but watch that cue.'

'Long grass him,' Kendrick bubbled.

Harry tried for the defensive shot, but the white hit another red and didn't come down the table. It rested against the right-hand cushion, just above the centre pocket. There was a red against the cushion opposite but higher up. Sherwill said:

'An easy little back double for you, John.'

Tucker hit the red on its right side. It came back smack into the centre pocket.

'Good shot,' said Harry.

'Good?' said Tucker. 'It was perfect.'

'Our President is a gifted player,' Sherwill observed. 'And modest with it.'

The white ball had come back to the right-hand side. The orange was on its spot with a line almost but not quite clear to the centre pocket.

'You will now see a shot' — Tucker wilted like the broken stalk of a dried-up daffodil — 'not often seen in this Club.'

There was a red just below the centre pocket, some inches from the cushion. Tucker hit the orange ball right of centre. It chipped the red and cannoned off into the pocket.

'You fluking toad,' said Sherwill.

'Balls,' said Tucker. 'A nominated shot.' He cued for a fairly simple red into the bottom right-hand pocket and missed by a couple of inches. 'Oh bugger.'

'That's more like it,' Sherwill said. 'That's the Tucker we know and love.'

Major Kendrick beamed at the two of them and at his guest.

Judith would be home by now with Peter, laying his tea, steeling herself for an hour's ordeal with the stubby-fingered lad from the harbour who wanted to learn to play 'Happy Days Are Here Again' in time for the Scout concert.

Harry thought of the way her hip stuck to his when they were close and wet and content, and of the sweet-sour smell of her throat.

Kendrick said: 'High time we got them on the run, Pearson.'

As the frame continued it was obvious that Tucker and Sherwill had played frequently together and automatically followed a certain course: Tucker went for the shots and occasionally got them, while Sherwill played almost everything safe. In the first fifteen minutes Harry had only two chances to pot: a difficult cut which he missed, and one lying over the top right-hand hole. He managed that but the white had an unlucky kiss, coming to rest behind another red with nothing but a long-distance view of the yellow. He had to play that, and for safety.

Tucker had a break of black and blue. Sherwill got an easy blue and missed a slightly trickier purple. With four reds left on the table, Harry and Kendrick were thirty-five points behind. The deficit was exaggerated by the higher-scoring balls, but it was a lot to make up. Then for the second time Sherwill slipped up and left Harry with a chance.

It was a long, fairly straight drive into the bottom left pocket. There were no colours near, and a distinct possibility of following through into the hole.

He took a chance and put plenty of top on.

The red spun in; the white came back, three-quarters the length of the table, to a good position on the purple.

Harry took the purple and with left-hand spin got his white on to a second red, lying close to one of the top pockets. The black was in position near the facing pocket but the shot on the red was very fine: too fine to hold the white. He put top on again and sent it up and down the table. The red went down, the black was on. He took it and got on his third red; from that on to the purple again. As it went down, hard and true, Kendrick gave a crow of delight:

'Never touched the sides! That makes thirty, and still to play.'

Another old skill, pulsing down into his fingers and then steadying where and when he needed it to steady. It took less than an hour to recapture this one. How long to make the same progress at the piano?

Or in learning to love again — love without wariness, without reservations?

The remaining red lay behind the baulk line, three inches from the left pocket and half obscured by the orange. Hitting it direct meant an almost certain in-off. Harry studied it for a moment. Then he played the white ball off two cushions, gently.

It came into the red from the rear, touched it, and rolled behind the orange, leaving a perfect snooker.

'Gawd,' said Sherwill.

'By George.' That was Major Kendrick. 'My dear chap.'

Harry said: 'A bit lucky.'

'There's no doubt about it,' said the President gloomily: 'the bugger's played before.' He gave Harry a respectful punch on the forearm, just hard enough to hurt. 'Come and have a noggin.'

'We're not open yet,' said Sherwill.

'I know we're not. Because you're barman tonight, and you're still fiddle-arsing about round here. What about opening up?'

Sherwill looked at his watch. 'I suppose it could be managed.'

Kendrick put one arm proprietorially around Harry's shoulders. They went through a scratched door with a loose, rattling handle into a room congested with armchairs, some covered in leather, some with washable covers which hadn't been washed for a long time. There was a noble fireplace, containing two long electric bars and a rise and fall of simulated flame.

It was like a far-flung, poverty-stricken, courageous outpost of St James's. Open a window, and you would look out on to alien territory.

Harry wondered how long it took Kendrick to shake off the atmosphere when he left. Did he walk boldly upright, alert and unrelaxed, through the strange streets until he was safe in his first-floor bed-sitter over the hall, at the fourpenny end of the town?

On the far side of the room was a shallow counter with a serving-hatch, its shutter held in place by a padlock.

'Hurrah,' growled a voice from the depths of a chair. 'Marines to the rescue, eh?'

'Early today,' said somebody else.

'Put a complaint in the suggestions box.'

Sherwill unfastened the hatch and pushed it upwards. He reached in and freed the flap. When he had squeezed through to the other side, the high counter cut him off at chest level, so that he appeared to be standing in a trench.

'What'll it be?' Tucker asked Harry.

'Do I hear our revered President offering pinkers?'

A man uncoiled himself from a chair, coming away from it with a faint creak and a plop. He was the same height as Tucker but broad with it. His oblong moustache looked as though it had been pasted on rather than grown.

'Ah, Duggie,' said Tucker. 'Duggie, friend of Kendrick's. Pearson. Sir Douglas Mallard.'

Two more members came forward and were introduced. Harry had passed both of them in the street at various times. Next time he could nod a greeting; but it would need a few more encounters before he got their names right.

He hadn't meant to meet people. Certainly he hadn't meant to let himself be drawn into their problems. But now, all at once, they were talking about the churchyard.

Looking back next day, he wouldn't recall who had started it. But they were all involved — all save for Mallard, who made a point of moving away to the far end of the room and putting his glass on a ledge above an old green-painted radiator.

'Going to spoil the whole look of the old place,' said Kendrick. 'Never know when to leave well alone. Same with everything nowadays.'

Sherwill tipped whisky into a measure, tipped the measure with amateurish care into the glass, and pushed it across the counter. 'Little busybodies in the town hall. Little twits who don't know an open space from a public bog. Can't stop meddling.'

'Sooner they reshuffle the boundaries and we come under Chedstowe, the better,' offered the man who was either Rickett or Proudfoot, Harry couldn't remember which.

The rest frowned, not prepared to go that far.

Tucker said: 'Doesn't seem to be any way of stopping them, once they get going.'

Nothing to do with me, said Harry inwardly. Don't belong here, won't be here much longer. No concern of mine.

Aloud he said: 'Have any of you been to inspect the plans? They ought to be available to the public, and the application for the Faculty ought to have been on the church door ages ago.'

'It's not,' said Tucker.

Proudfoot, or maybe Rickett, said: 'I heard they were going to keep the headstones and lay them to form a new path.'

'Get trodden to bits.'

'Always thought once you'd bought your plot, paid for it, all that, you had it for keeps. Dammit, if they can come digging you up or chucking your stones down for anyone to trample on, what's it all about — how're they going to find us on Judgment Day, hey?'

'Give me cremation.'

'Gladly.'

'Decent burial at sea.'

'We get enough poisonous things washed up on the beach as it is.'

'Pearson, you're not drinking very fast. Come on, let's have your glass.'

Harry said: 'Is there such a thing as a town historian?'

'Old whatsit,' said Tucker.

'Old Hodge-Hargreaves,' Sherwill expanded. 'Used to look after the sailors'' museum until it fell down. Keeps the bits in his back room now.'

'He'd know about the churchyard and the local families buried there?'

'Ought to have been there himself, long ago. Must be ninety if he's a day.'

'There's something about a hundred-year rule,' said Harry. 'I don't think they can tamper with any burial which has taken place within the last hundred years. Maybe they can get special dispensation on that — but not, I'm pretty sure, if there are any members of the family still living and they care to complain.'

The others looked around, as though hoping someone would come in knowing all the answers.

'Any architects among us?' Harry asked.

'My wife's brother has a practice in Norwich.'

'Maybe he'd be prepared to advise on the likely deterioration of stones laid flat underfoot.'

'Experts,' said Major Kendrick approvingly into his whisky. 'Yes. Absolutely.'

'It's no good just grumbling,' said

Harry. 'And no good flailing wildly in all directions. You need a coordinator — or at any rate a coordinating group. Some properly organised team that the public know about, that they can approach, before it's too late. Let the town council see you mean business. You need a solicitor, an architect, some local figure who's respected by — '

'Been in the district long?' asked Mallard brusquely from the other end of the room.

'Only a few weeks.'

'Some kind of preservationist?'

'I'm . . . ' He thought of the briefest way of putting it. 'A job analyst,' he said.

'Hm. One of those.'

'You're right,' said Kendrick eagerly. 'Damn sure you're right, Pearson . . . Harry. When those blighters get busy, you have to hit 'em with all you've got. An expert on one side, expert on another — then wham, a frontal attack in strength.'

'Try it in there one day.' Tucker nodded towards the snooker room.

'There ought to be a rota of inquirers at the town hall' — Harry was carried away — 'demanding as ratepayers to see the plans. Some responsible person must write a letter asking for declaration of the terms of the Faculty granted — if any. There's the Dilapidations Commission . . .'

'How busy are you at the moment?' asked Tucker.

'I'm only a visitor.' Caught in mid flight, he came down to earth.

Mallard, far away, snorted meaninglessly.

'So you're unbiased,' said Tucker. 'And you seem to know all the ins and outs.'

'No. But I do know that you have to analyse the thing in advance, give people specific jobs, and pull the results together.'

'You're nominated,' said Tucker.

'Oh, but — '

'I'll rope in Hodge-Hargreaves. Timmy, get your wife to give her brother a tinkle. I suggest a meeting tomorrow afternoon. If we want to stop that lot in time — '

'First thing,' said Harry, 'is to slap an injunction on them. Hold things up until everyone's had a chance of looking at what the consequences are likely to be.'

'If you say so. Look, do you think perhaps first thing in the morning you could drop in . . . '

When Major Kendrick walked proudly away with his guest, Harry said:

'I didn't mean to get lumbered with all that. I ought to have kept my mouth shut.'

'Livened the place up no end.' They walked down High Street, utterly deserted, with few lights in the closed shops.

'Oh, and . . . er,' said Kendrick awkwardly, 'don't pay too much attention to Duggie Mallard.'

'He had every right to ask what business it was of mine. After all, he lives here and I don't.'

'Lives miles away, actually. Family used to own half the county. His father lost a packet on the gee-gees, but Duggie still thinks he ought to own the lot of us. Good type, really. But you don't have to let him upset you.'

They were only a couple of streets away from Judith's house.

Kendrick said: 'We have a three-month membership for visitors. You know, use the Club. Only a couple of guineas. If you did want to join, I — '

'It's very kind of you,' said Harry, 'but I haven't got three months left.'

'Oh well. Only a couple of guineas,' the major urged. He shot Harry a bright, shy glance. 'You have to go by Easter?'

'That's my deadline.'

Deadline. Not a happy word.

Kendrick cleared his throat, went pinker than usual, and said gruffly: 'Mrs. Marshall won't like that.'

'She'll have many more promising pupils than me.'

'She's a nice girl. Lovely girl.'

'Yes.'

'She's had a pretty rough time,' said Kendrick. He was quite fierce.

'Yes,' said Harry, 'I know.'

They understood each other.

★   ★   ★

She had been lying on her back, but now turned towards him again, into his arms. They made love again, more tenderly and languidly this time, and then lay side by side and stared again at the cobweb of grey cracks in the uneven ceiling. Sleet

213

whipped for a few furious seconds against the window of the smokehouse. The sound of the sea was gruff and steady here.

He let his hand lie on her smooth flank; and was at peace.

She spoilt it, without meaning to. She said: 'Now I suppose you want to dash out and get on with your coordinating?'

'Mm?' He had only half-heard her, still lapped in the lazy pleasure of having her beside him.

'You're not thinking about me.' She stroked his shoulder. 'You'd sooner be out there organising the rebels, wouldn't you?'

She had come straight here after seeing Peter to school, and now it was only mid-morning. Body and mind he had been aware of nothing but Judith. Now she had broken the spell: he found himself wondering if that chap Barber had got the catalogues of new rotary cutters yet, and whether the solicitor had devised just the right sort of letter to elicit costings which the defensive town council still pleaded could not be broken down.

He said: 'They can manage without me for a while.'

'You've certainly got caught up in poor old Ormeswich, haven't you?'

The idyll had never stood a chance of lasting on a purely ethereal plane. From the moment he arrived he must subconsciously have been analysing the flow of the town and its people. Every community had its own tempo and its own pattern. You couldn't make yourself not notice. No professional could discard his training and opt for innocence — once that's gone, you can't decide you'd have been better off sticking to it.

'Speaking of old Ormeswich,' he said, 'do you think Mrs. Ainsworth has any relatives in the churchyard? She must have a few ancestors there. Maybe we could get her to lodge a protest on behalf of the family.'

Judith shook her head, her hair spilling across his chest. 'I don't fancy Mrs. Ainsworth'll want to discuss churchyards. Outliving the other old dear down the coast is all she's concerned with now. Graves are the last thing . . . '

If you want to be a dropout, you have to drop the whole way. Commit yourself to any kind of work, and you're sunk.

'Come back to me,' Judith whispered. It was not coquettish but direct, urgent, loving.

When she left, hurrying off to have an early lunch and then give a lesson to the girls in a small private school on the parade, he felt a sickening sense of loss. He wanted to run after her and force her to come back. Wild promises were on the tip of his tongue.

Once you start living, you're in greater danger of dying.

Arlene had been more beautiful. Arlene could afford to keep herself beautiful. As a matter of pride she had been sexually inventive, and as a matter of pride she expected him to make love to her at reasonable intervals. He had suspected that somewhere she chalked up a score: if he let three or four nights go by, there would be sly sneers — feeling tired, life getting too much for you? — but then, when he had been goaded into desiring her, her triumph was in lying sullen and unaccepting.

And yet . . .

No. No, he wasn't going to turn the past over and over between his fingers. There had been too many complications. With Judith there were no complications: nothing that wasn't simple and natural and joyful.

Until Easter.

It was as though she were still in the room with him and had said it to his face, he heard it so clearly.

At lunchtime he went up to the *Galleon* and had sandwiches and a couple of pints in the public bar. The landlord still called him Mr. Pearson, but a fisherman in the corner, who had twice told him lengthy stories about comic disasters of the past, unexpectedly called him Harry this morning and, with a nod, suggested a fill-up.

By the middle of the afternoon he was standing in the doorway of the smoke-house in spite of gusts of wind that carried intermittent sleet. It was too early for Judith to come and collect Peter yet, but he wanted to stand here and wait for her. He'd intercept her, they'd meet Peter together, walk back — play, or talk, for a while before he and Kendrick went to the Club to see how the campaign was progressing.

A woman came down the steps and looked over the sand towards him. Something about the set of her head was familiar. But then, so many people were familiar to him now — by sight, even when names and faces were not yet linked.

She saw him, and stared. Then she stepped down from the end of the promenade and walked towards the smokehouse. Her stride was long for a woman's; she didn't pick her way, or flounder over patches of pebbles and more tightly packed hummocks.

He knew now who it was.

She reached the doorway and looked into his face as though prepared to believe, at this last moment, that there might just possibly be some mistake. She had to be quite sure before she spoke.

He rammed his hand against the warped edge of the door, where a few splinters were beginning to shred away.

Arlene said: 'So you didn't have the guts to go through with it.'

8

The inquest was held in the council chamber of the town hall. The coroner sat in an oak chair in front of the empty mayoral chair, with the members of the jury in the seats normally used by aldermen and councillors.

The coroner was Mr. Cyril Wratten, whose solicitor's practice in High Street was five doors from the Godyll club. He was a member of the Club and had been giving his services free in the campaign against the proposed churchyard alterations. Having sat on the protest committee with Harry Pearson, he now had to adjust to Harry Pearson being Harold Grant.

Stiffly he addressed the jury. They were here to inquire into the death of Mrs. Harold Grant. Evidence to be presented today would show that the deceased had died an unnatural death.

'Since police investigations into the

responsibility for this death are still progressing, it will not be possible for us to record a verdict today. I propose merely to establish identity and the physical cause of death, and then to adjourn until such time as it may be necessary to recall you.'

The coroner's officer called Harold Grant.

There was a rustle on the public benches. Heads turned; eyes and ears waited greedily.

'You are Harold Grant?'

'Yes.'

'Your present address is The Smokehouse, South Shore, Ormeswich?'

'It is.'

'Is that your permanent address?'

'No.'

'Will you please give the court your permanent address.'

'I don't have one. I left it some weeks ago.'

The coroner looked down at the papers on the ledge before him. He said: 'You are being very meticulous, Mr. Grant. Would it be correct to say that before you came to Ormeswich your address, as shown on your personal documents, and at which you resided with the late Mrs. Grant, was The Paddocks, Helming Hill, Buckinghamshire?'

'That is correct.'

'Thank you. Now, Mr. Pears . . . Mr. Grant . . . have you identified the body shown to you in Chedstowe mortuary?'

'I have.'

'Will you tell the jury whose body it was?'

'My wife. Arlene Marguerite Grant.'

'When did you last see your wife alive?'

'On the morning of Thursday the 17th of February.'

'Can you give me a closer idea of the time?'

'She came to the smokehouse to see me at about 10 a.m., and left about 11.30.'

'You didn't see her again that day?'

'I didn't see her again until I was . . . sent for. Taken to the mortuary.'

There was a buzz of disappointment as he stood down. The audience had been hoping for some high drama.

The next witness was the police surgeon. He gave his findings as though reciting an especially dull and obvious page from a textbook. The death blow had been administered by a heavy blade of some kind capable of shattering the cranium and driving two inches into the brain, forming a gash of four inches from front to rear. A spade had been found near the body. It lay on the table before the jury, with a ticket round its haft as though newly bought from an ironmonger's; but it wasn't new — it was stained with earth and mud and other things.

From samples of blood and tufts of hair taken from the spade, the surgeon was prepared to say that it was the murder weapon.

After being struck, the deceased had either fallen or been pushed over the cliff near the south-eastern wall of the church-yard and, as contusions and tearings of the skin on temples, cheeks and jaw showed, had landed face down on the beach. The force of the impact, added the surgeon, intent on making two women members of the jury turn paler than they already were, had considerably widened the cleft in the skull.

The spade had been thrown down after her.

Death must have taken place in something under two hours before he was called to the scene. He had arrived at 6.45 p.m. It was unlikely that death could have occurred much before 5 p.m.

A workman, defensive yet enjoying his ordeal, identified the spade as one that he had been using on Thursday the 17th of February. They had knocked off early that day and left their tools in the churchyard because someone had come with some sort of paper to stop them digging up anything more until they were given an official go-ahead.

Mr. Wratten, who had been instrumental in having that injunction served, nodded. 'Yes, quite. Yes.'

Picks and spades had been stacked under a small lean-to against the churchyard wall. No, they didn't always take their tools away with them: Ormeswich wasn't a place where folk pinched things.

'And anyway, knocking off unexpected like that, there wasn't no lorry to pick us up, and we weren't going to hump 'em home with us.'

The three who had found the body were called. The coroner disliked them so much that, leaning over backwards to disguise his prejudices, he was downright effusive. They began to enjoy themselves and regretted the briefness of their formal report of discovery and the approximate time: it was established that it couldn't have been more than a few minutes after 6 p.m., since they had heard the hour striking as they came along the beach.

The entire proceedings had taken less than a quarter of an hour. The coroner asked that anyone who could shed light on any aspect of the case should get in touch with the police and, if the inquest were resumed later, should come forward and give evidence there. He was prepared to take note of local opinion as well as specific facts, and of hearsay evidence.

He then adjourned the inquest *sine die*.

* * *

The widower and his brother-in-law lunched together at the *White Hart*. Neither of them ate a great deal. The waitress on their table reported snippets of their conversation back to the kitchen.

'Do you realise what it cost . . . ?'

The bigger man was doing most of the talking. At one stage he said with considerable force:

'After all that bloody mess you made for us, you're right in it yourself, now, aren't you? In one hell of a mess, Harold.'

Before leaving Ormeswich he was asked if he could spare an hour or so to help the police in their inquiries.

★　★　★

The detective-inspector said: 'I see from the statement you gave to your local police two days ago that Mrs. Grant left Helming Hill on the morning of Wednesday the 16th of February. Early in the morning?'

'Can't vouch for the exact time of departure. I live fifteen miles away. But we'd settled the night before that she should drive down, and I imagine she got away in good time.'

'Were there any . . . special circumstances . . . connected with this visit?'

'Plenty,' said Norman Leggett crossly. And he said just as crossly: 'I've already gone over this with our local people. About how he walked out, and the time it took us to find him . . . and now this.'

'Yes, sir. It was very helpful of you. It's all been passed on to us. But there are one or two points I'd like to go over with you personally.'

'Go on, let's have it.'

'Was there anything to lead you to suppose Mrs. Grant would be in any danger when she got here?'

'You don't think I'd have let her come if I'd thought that?'

'I gather from your earlier statements that until she identified him, neither of you were sure that the man here would turn out to be Mr. Grant at all.'

'We weren't sure, no.'

'So she might have found herself facing a dangerous criminal.'

'My sister,' said Norman Leggett, 'was

226

a very determined woman. And she knew what she was doing. If the man had been a crook, she wouldn't have let on who she was, but reported back to me. Then we'd have decided where we went from there.' He slammed a large hand heavily down on his knee. 'But anyway, it was Harold. And where does that leave us?'

'Exactly. Where? Mr. Leggett . . . do you know of anyone with any reason for wishing your sister's death?'

After an aching few seconds, Norman Leggett said:

'What are you asking me to say?'

'Anything you think you ought to say, sir.'

There was a longer silence. The inspector himself had to break it. He ventured:

'Going back to this business of Mr. Grant clearing off — had he and Mrs. Grant quarrelled?'

'Not really. I mean, not over anything special.'

'You mean that in general they weren't on good terms?'

'He'd been so depressed. You couldn't get through to him. It was his bankruptcy last year, he took it hard, couldn't see it was all in the game. We tried to cheer him up — keep things going the way they always had been, till he was on his feet again. But he wouldn't play.'

'And then he walked out without a word. No warning.'

'None.'

'No note, or anything?'

'Not a thing,' said Norman Leggett firmly. 'We were worried stiff. Thought he might have done something stupid.'

'Yes, sir. I believe you reported your fears to . . . ' The detective turned a sheet of paper over. 'Inspector Brewer.'

'Fat lot of attention he paid.'

'He discounted the theory of suicide.'

'Never gave it a second thought.'

'Rightly, as it appears.' Before Norman Leggett could find a retort, the detective went on: 'When Mrs. Grant had established that the man living here under an assumed name was her husband, did she intend to ask him to come home? Do you know if they had a scene . . . or anything?'

'Arlene rang me that evening, after she'd seen him.'

'This would be Wednesday the 16th?'

'Right. She'd seen Harold that afternoon. Wanted him to come home, and be looked after, and talk things over. And he didn't want to know. He told her he'd got out and he intended to stay out.'

'Did he say what he intended to do when his money ran out?'

'I asked Arlene that. She said it was scaring, the way he wouldn't discuss it. She said . . . '

'Yes, Mr. Leggett?'

'She said it was insulting, the real rejection in his face when he saw her. That's what she said it was: out-and-out rejection. All those years of marriage, and now this brush-off. It was rough.'

'How rough? Rough enough,' said the inspector, 'for Mr. Grant to want to kill her?'

'I didn't say — '

'No, Mr. Leggett. You didn't. But nobody else in Ormeswich knew Mrs. Grant, did they? She was a stranger here, the only person who had any connection with her was her husband — who'd walked out on her and didn't want to go back.'

'It could have been . . . oh, you know, one of those aimless killings. There's a hell of a lot of violence about.'

'Aimless?'

'Those hippies. The three who say they just happened to find Arlene on the beach. What about them?'

The inspector sat back and studied him. 'Mr. Leggett, there's something about which you don't seem able to make up your mind.'

'I don't get you.'

'I don't get it myself,' said the inspector wearily. After a moment he went on; 'That man you sent to find Mr. Grant — was he still around on that Wednesday and Thursday?'

'My sister told him to leave as soon as she'd established that it was Harold.'

'And then, on her own, she saw Mr. Grant again on the Thursday?'

'I'd told her on the phone, the night before, to get him back somehow. There was a lot to be tidied up. Harold was always so methodical himself — he of all people ought to have seen that. She was to see him again on the Thursday, get him to see sense . . . '

'But you never heard the outcome of that meeting?'

'No.'

'No idea whether Mrs. Grant may have provoked him in any way — lost her temper?'

'I wouldn't blame her if she had.'

'Nor would I, Mr. Leggett. But if, as you say, Mr. Grant was in a disturbed state of mind, and resentful about her arrival and any plans you may have had for him — '

'A disturbed state of mind,' said Norman Leggett. 'That's about the size of it. It was disturbed when he walked out, and I think it still is.'

'You don't really think it was the three hippies, after all?'

The inspector's faint irony went unnoticed.

'Whatever the truth may be, whatever did happen and whatever he did . . . if it was Harold who did anything . . . I don't think he could have known what he was doing. I should never' — he bowed his head in remorse — 'have let Arlene come down here on her own. I see that now.'

* * *

The spade carried clear fingerprints of the workman who had been using it on the day of the killing, and some smudgier ones of two of his mates. Certain smears over these prints made it seem probable that the killer had worn gloves.

* * *

It was the third time Harold Grant had been questioned. They went over the same ground each time, waiting for a discrepancy to pop out.

'The smokehouse must be a cold place at this time of year,' said the detective-inspector.

'I spend a lot of time out walking.'

'That can be pretty cold, too. You wear gloves?'

'I didn't bring any with me.'

'You haven't bought a pair since you've been here?'

'No.'

'The night you left home — '

'Was a cold one,' Harold Grant finished for him. 'Yes. But I didn't intend to be

232

walking around for long. I was carrying some letters, I didn't pick up my gloves, I just went out.'

'And didn't go back.'

'As you say, I didn't go back.'

'Mr. Grant, you say you didn't intend to be walking around for long. When we last talked' — he consulted his notes — 'you told me you had decided to leave home and have a long holiday while you sorted out certain personal and business problems in your mind. Which,' he conceded, 'you had of course every right to do. But when you say you didn't intend to be walking around for long, do you mean — well, were you referring to catching a train, or a bus, or a taxi: is that it?'

Harold Grant hesitated. Then he said: 'I may as well tell you.'

'I'd be glad if you would.'

'I had intended to commit suicide.'

The inspector drew a deep breath. 'So Mr. Leggett wasn't so far wrong — and your wife — when they suspected that that was what was in your mind when you went out. It didn't happen; but it was a close thing.'

'They had every reason to believe that was what had happened, after the letters I'd written them.'

'Letters?'

'The letters I was taking to the post. That's what was in them — the whole story.'

'But Mr. Leggett and Mrs. Grant both denied having received any suicide notes at the time.'

'How very interesting.'

'You're sure you posted them, Mr. Grant? You were obviously very upset that evening.'

'My wife referred to them when she came to Ormeswich. They led to some acrimonious discussion.'

'That's very odd.'

'Isn't it?'

'You say it was one of the subjects you discussed, but — '

'But she can't confirm it now. No, I see that.'

The inspector groped for a firmer hold. 'You say your original intention was to commit suicide. But you changed your mind.'

'I . . . postponed it.'

'Until when?'

'*Sine die.*' It was a mocking echo of the coroner's adjournment.

'How did you propose to do it?'

'By shooting myself.'

'Really?' Suddenly the inspector lunged: 'Do you still have the gun?'

Harold Grant bit his lip. 'Blast. Forget it.'

'I'm afraid not, Mr. Grant. Do you still have it?'

'Yes.'

'On your person at the moment?'

'In the smokehouse.'

'Do you have a firearm certificate?' When there was no reply: 'Do you, Mr. Grant?'

'No.'

'I shall have to ask you to hand the weapon in. And of course there are likely to be proceedings.'

'But I may want it . . . '

'Want it? What for, sir?' Another silence. 'You're not still thinking of doing away with yourself, are you?' Still no response. The detective-inspector allowed a good twenty or thirty seconds, then said: 'When Mrs. Grant left you on that Thursday morning, did she give any indication of what she would be doing the rest of the day? Was she going to set out for home?'

'Not immediately. There was some talk of our going back to Helming Hill together. Maybe the next day.'

'You were definitely going to go back with her?'

'It wasn't at all definite. Not so far as I was concerned.'

'You were angry with Mrs. Grant for facing you with such a decision? Angry with her for finding you at all?'

'It was just that I'd sooner not have been disturbed.'

'You wished to remain in Ormeswich incognito.'

'I wanted time to think things over before . . . '

'Yes, Mr. Grant?' The detective-inspector waited, then leaned forward. He was a plump man, with a fleshy face which ought to have been cheerful but had grown lugubrious over the disillusioning years. 'You were prepared to commit violence against yourself, but not against Mrs. Grant?'

'I had a gun. But I didn't shoot her.'

'We know that.'

'And as for bashing her head in with . . . the thought of . . . ' He couldn't go on.

'Can you tell me of anyone with reason to kill Mrs. Grant?'

'Of course I can't.'

'She knew nobody in Ormeswich but you?'

'Nobody, I'm sure.'

'There was nobody else who might have wanted her . . . out of the way?'

'Who could there have been?'

'Did anyone else know she would be here on that day — those two days?'

'I can't think of anyone. Apart from her brother, and maybe his wife . . . maybe his secretary. Oh, and Norman's pet bloodhound, of course.'

'Who had left by the Thursday.'

'Had he? I wouldn't know.'

An American fighter plane from some inland base screamed low overhead, making conversation impossible. As its howl drooped through a succession of semitones across the sky, another came clamouring after it. Then there was only the dull, unending background throb of the sea.

'Mr. Grant, you've been spending quite some time in the company of Mrs. Judith Marshall.'

'What's that got to do with it?'

'We have to take every factor into consideration.'

'I've been taking piano lessons from Mrs. Marshall.'

'An odd thing, for someone so recently contemplating suicide.'

'It's not the only odd thing in this case.'

'Your friendship with Mrs. Marshall — '

'Leave her out of it. None of this can possibly have anything to do with Mrs. Marshall, so leave her right out of it.'

'Am I right in supposing that she knew you only as Harry Pearson?'

'To start with, yes.'

'When did she learn that your name was Grant, and that there was a Mrs. Grant?'

'Why don't you ask her?'

'We intend to. I was hoping to have

your own comment first.'

'Inspector, haven't you overlooked one important part of your ritual?'

'Ritual, sir?'

'All these questions, and hints, and accusations — '

'Nobody's accusing you of anything, sir.'

'You're putting up a damn good impersonation of someone doing just that, then. Oughtn't you to caution me, or something?'

'Nobody is cautioned, sir, unless he is about to be charged with a crime.'

'And you're not charging me — yet?'

'I'm simply asking for your voluntary co-operation in sorting out this distressing business, sir.'

Harold Grant gave every sign of subsiding into stubborn muteness. Then, resignedly, he said: 'All right. Mrs. Marshall didn't know the whole truth until that Wednesday, after I'd seen my wife.'

'Thank you, sir.'

'But it still has nothing to do with this case. Leave her alone — do you hear me?'

'Yes, Mr. Grant; I hear you.'

The cremation was attended by the dead woman's husband, their two children, her brother, her brother's secretary and five friends. The friends were austerely loyal but disapproving. In their world, people got divorced, had abortions, occasionally had the bad luck to run somebody over, and were known to get the occasional black eye or glass of gin in the face at parties; but didn't get brutally murdered.

The friends looked at Harold and looked away.

His two children looked at him and then stared off into the middle distance.

Harold, appraising the mourners, said: 'Veronica wasn't up to it?'

'She's inside,' said Norman flatly.

'In . . . ' He looked into the square, antiseptic chapel.

'In for the cure. The usual place. For the twentieth time.'

They went in. The ceremony was brisk and impersonal. There were four names on the day's programme before Arlene's, and when they came out cars were already driving up for the next disposal.

Amanda forced herself to come closer to her father.

'You'll be coming home with us?'

'I think I'd better get back to Ormeswich. Sort a few things out.'

Their relief was pitifully obvious.

Norman said: 'They're staying with me for the time being. Welcome as long as they want to stay.'

The two men moved down the path. The others fell away into different groups.

'I'm sorry about Veronica,' said Harold.

'So you bloody well should be. If it hadn't been for that load of slop you dished out in your letter, she wouldn't have drunk herself into — '

'So Veronica's letter arrived,' said Harold sardonically.

'It arrived, all right.'

'Funny about the other two.'

'What other two?'

'The ones you told the police you'd never received.'

'Because I didn't — '

'Arlene told me. When she came down.

241

You got them, those letters. You and Arlene — '

'I'm talking about Veronica. She'd never show us her letter, but I know it knocked her over.'

'All I said in it was — '

'I don't want to know. Whatever you said, it was the way she took it. Getting her all gooey-eyed, all drooling over her lost love gone for ever — Godawlmighty!'

'It wasn't like that. I wrote nothing like that at all.'

'Whatever you wrote, she read plenty into it. And went off after you into cloud cuckoo land. A pity you didn't cart her off with you instead of dumping a load of half-witted sentimental drivel on her.'

Harold said: 'Norman. Listen to me. There was precious little in that letter. Nothing for anyone to get steamed up about. I had a few minutes, I thought there wasn't long to go, I'd always been sorry for Veronica — '

'You? You've got the nerve to be sorry for Veronica? She could have done without that. She's always been a darned sight too sorry for herself, without you cheering her on.'

'You treat her abominably,' said Harold. 'And you know it, and I know it. Everybody knows it.'

'So Sir Bloody Galahad has to start meddling.'

'She felt at ease with me — we got on, I liked her — and that's the lot. And that's all there was in that letter. Thanking her for her friendship, wishing her all the best, saying I was sorry for what I was going to do, but hoping she'd understand.'

'Understand? I'll tell you what she understood: that you'd been harbouring a secret passion for her for years, and this was the tragic bloody end.'

'Oh. God, no.'

'Oh, God, yes. And what do you think it was like,' said Norman vehemently, 'when she found you weren't dead after all?'

9

A faltering rendition of *Für Elise* seeped across the street, dulled by the closed window, slow to start with and still slower when the left-hand phrases came fumbling through.

'Ought to be ashamed of herself. Carrying on as though nothing had happened.'

'Carrying on — that's just about it.'

'I'm not letting my Shirley go there any more.'

'Mind you, nothing was said about her at the inquest.'

'They want to keep it quiet, that's what. You'll see. They'll be working on it.'

'Reckon he won't have been the first, this Pearson or Grant or whatever.'

'Not by a long sight he won't.'

'You ask me, her husband died just at the right time, poor lad.'

'He was all right, was young Jim.'

'Oh, Jim was all right. Worked himself

to the bone for that house. Left her nicely, thank you. And now look at her. You can't tell me that all these years she hasn't been . . . '

A man cut across their path, crossed the road, went up to the front door and rang the bell.

'That's not him, is it?'

'One of them plainclothes lot. I've seen him around, asking questions.'

'About time too.'

The hobbling notes stopped. The front door opened.

'Anyway, my Shirley's not going there any more, I've settled that.'

When the little boy had gone, clutching his music case and glancing apprehensively at the detective-sergeant, Judith said:

'I don't really see how I can help you.'

'We're trying to establish everybody's movements on Thursday the 17th of February.'

It was a date she knew she would never forget. The day itself, and the death-knell repetition ever since: Thursday the 17th of February, Thursday the 17th of

February, Thursday the . . .

'Everybody's?' she said.

'We'd particularly like your confirmation of Mr. Harold Grant's whereabouts on the afternoon of Mrs. Grant's death.'

'I'm sure he's already told you.'

'Yes, Mrs. Marshall. But we'd appreciate your corroboration.'

There was nothing to be afraid of. The truth was steady enough. It was the answer to whatever they might be thinking. But if there were some small discrepancy between her story and Harry's, would that stir up trouble? She'd heard of innocent men being arrested before now; even of them being convicted.

She said: 'Are you accusing Mr. Grant — '

'Nobody's being accused of anything,' said the detective-sergeant. 'And the more people we can eliminate, the less likelihood there is of the wrong man being accused.'

It might have been meant as an answer to her unspoken doubts.

'I went to collect my son from school,' she said. 'At the usual time, about half past three. As we came away, Harry — '

'Mr. Grant?'

'I . . . yes.'

'You know him better as Mr. Pearson. Harry Pearson.'

If that was a question, she didn't see that she was called on to reply. She said: 'Harry met us, and we came here.'

'Right away?'

'It's a ten-minute walk. We came straight here, and Peter had his tea, while we talked.'

'Had you anything special to talk about: anything related to this case?'

'Harry . . . Mr. Grant . . . said he might have to go back home the following day.'

'He was intending to leave Ormeswich?'

'Just to settle some outstanding business. It wasn't definite, even, that he'd go.' She remembered him, wretchedly arguing to and fro, thinking aloud at her and waiting for her to come up with a simple solution. But there hadn't been any simple solution; and she was still dazed by all that he'd told her the day before. 'In any case,' she said, 'he had no intention of going back permanently.'

'That's what he promised you?'

'It wasn't a matter of promising me anything. We . . . just talked.'

'And when he left?'

'He had arranged to meet Mrs. Grant again that evening.'

'And drive back with her?'

'Perhaps the next day.'

'Mrs. Grant hadn't booked in for another night at the hotel.'

'I don't know anything about that. I just know that when he left here he was going to meet her.'

'What time did he leave here?'

'It must have been getting on for six.'

'Six o'clock?'

'Somewhere between half past five and six.'

'You're sure of that, Mrs. Marshall?'

'Yes.'

The detective looked impassive, but she felt that here he had been hoping for some little slip. If the times hadn't tallied, he would have pounced. But why shouldn't they tally? If she told the same story as Harry's, it was because they were both telling the truth.

'And all that time,' he said, 'you were just talking.'

'For the last fifteen minutes or so we played the piano.'

'Played the piano?' he said incredulously.

'There were a couple of duets we were fond of. We felt like playing them. That's all.'

He must be dying to ask her a dozen questions, but wasn't sure which were relevant and which weren't. Judith herself wasn't sure. What would anyone make of people who sat at the piano, four hands on a keyboard, at a time like that? Sentimental farewell; or crazy pretence that everything was normal — shutting out reality with a barrage of sound?

'You couldn't have been mistaken about the time?'

She had been drawn back so completely into those moments when they sat there in the last cadence of the music, slowing it down because when it was finished Harry would have to go, that for an instant she thought the question must be concerned with the tempo. She shook herself back into the present and said:

'No.'

There was a shuffle of footsteps in the passage. The detective-sergeant's head turned.

'Of course.' It hadn't occurred to her before. 'Major Kendrick was in. He must have heard us. He'll tell you. He lives by the clock — he's not likely to make a mistake.'

She hurried to the door before the major could let himself out of the front door.

He looked round at her with the rather awkward, withdrawn expression he'd had since Harry Pearson had been publicly shown to be Harold Grant. She hated to ask him a favour: they had been no more than timidly polite to each other these last few days. But she said:

'Major Kendrick, I hate to ask you, but I wonder . . . '

'Yes, my dear?'

He couldn't help sounding nice about it. He hadn't got out of the habit of calling her 'my dear'.

'There's a detective-sergeant here,' she

said. 'He wants to settle the time that Harry left here that day — that Thursday.'

'Oh.' The blue eyes clouded. 'That Thursday. Yes.'

Reluctantly he came into the room.

Judith said: 'Major Kendrick, perhaps you'll confirm that Harry couldn't have left here before — '

'Please, Mrs. Marshall!' The detective cut in hurriedly. 'I'd prefer you to let me ask the question in my own way.'

'I'm sorry.'

Kendrick faced the inquisitor.

'You were in the house, sir, on the afternoon of Thursday the 17th of February?'

'I was.'

'Do you know what time Mrs. Marshall came in, and whether there was anyone with her?'

'Usual time, of course. Went to school to fetch the boy, got here the same as usual. Round about a quarter to four, I'd say.'

'There was just her son with her?'

'I don't go peeking out of windows or listening at keyholes,' said Kendrick, 'but it's a small house. I did hear a man's voice as well.'

251

'Not the boy's?'

'Not the boy's,' said the major contemptuously. 'Much deeper.'

'You recognised the voice?'

'I didn't go out of my way to recognise it. If I'd been asked — '

'I am asking you, Major. If you can possibly be definite.'

'Couldn't be definite, no. But I took it that it was Harry Pearson. Only his name's Grant, isn't it? Anyway, he came here on his own quite often, let himself into the house, practised. And came for lessons when Mrs. Marshall was here.'

'Did it sound as though he was having a lesson that afternoon?'

'Sounded more as though they were enjoying themselves. Playing a couple of tunes they'd played a lot. Not much of an ear for music, myself, but I remembered them.'

'What time would this be, sir?'

Major Kendrick hauled out his watch and flipped open the cover. He consulted it earnestly as though doing so would jog his memory.

'Getting on for half past five,' he said.

'Just before I went out.'

'You went out?'

'I had to go to a meeting at the Club. Pearson . . . Grant, I mean . . . he was supposed to be there too, but I didn't like to interrupt, and — '

'So you don't know what time he left?'

'All I know is it couldn't have been before half past five,' said Major Kendrick firmly.

'Thank you, sir.' Then, as the major reached the door, the detective said: 'One thing, sir — you're sure it was a duet you heard?'

'I beg your pardon?'

'Both Mrs. Marshall and Mr. Grant were playing? It couldn't just have been one of them?'

'What the devil are you driving at?'

'You're quite sure, sir, that Mr. Grant couldn't have left without your hearing him, and that Mrs. Marshall was playing the piano on her own, after he'd gone?'

Kendrick glared. His cheeks were mottled. Judith wanted to say she was sorry, she didn't want him mixed up in this. It had ruined everything.

Kendrick said: 'I've told you, I'm no musician. But I knew they liked duets, and I heard those two over and over again through the floor, and the stuff sounded the same to me. I don't know if you can make a solo out of a duet. Haven't the foggiest. But it sounded as though a lot was going on — all the usual notes, or whatever.'

'Thank you, sir.'

This time the major was allowed to escape. When he had gone, the detective-sergeant looked sheepishly down at his notes.

Judith said: 'That was a pretty dirty suggestion, wasn't it?'

'I have to ask, ma'am.'

'I hope you're satisfied.' When he didn't respond, she said: 'Now I think you'd better go.'

'There were one or two more things I wanted to ask.'

'I've told you all I know.'

'If we have to contact you again — '

'You'll be wasting your time. Because there's nothing else to say.'

She showed him out. It took her five

minutes to stop trembling.

After lunch she waited for her pupil. An hour's misery before she could go and meet Harry. The girl was a trier: she really worked, and longed to be told she was making good progress; but she was such a plodder, with so little spark.

Judith sat and waited in the chair in the window. She had been sitting here that Wednesday when Harry came to tell her about Arlene and the rest of it.

She could see him as he was in the dusk of that afternoon, standing on the step. His face had shrunk in on itself. The laughter in his eyes had drained away.

He said: 'I've got something to tell you.'

'Bad?' she said.

He nodded. She had always known somehow, somewhere deep down, that he would sooner or later have something bad to tell her.

So it was to be now.

He told her everything. Or she supposed it was everything. About the tide on which he'd let himself drift, about his self-disgust, and about the suicide that wasn't. There was no self-pity in the recital: scorn for himself all the way, but no pity. At one stage, her heart pounding as though she was living through the agony with him, she had said: 'You don't have to take all the blame, do you? I mean, if you were driven to that kind of desperation, the others did their fair share of driving.' But he wanted to listen to no excuses. He wasn't going to list grudges and petty resentments. He was here now, the way he was, because of the accumulation of things he had done and things he had failed to do.

And now Arlene was here as well.

She couldn't question him about Arlene. She had known all along that there had to be an Arlene in the background, but she had prevented herself from thinking too hard about it. If Harry now accused himself of cheating by living in an uncritical, unquestioning lull, she had helped him to cheat.

'I'm not going to trot out the old 'my wife doesn't understand me' rigmarole' — he was implacable — 'and I'm not a henpecked husband or some mawkish romantic with the seven-year itch, or any other periodic itch. At least, I hope I'm not.'

'You've got a lot to say about what you're not,' she observed, still trying to get her bearings and control her dizziness. There was too much to cope with all at once. 'What about what you *are*?'

Peter in the next room had eaten his tea and turned on the television. Upstairs Major Kendrick bumped about. And she and Harry talked, and he said, 'I love you, Judith, and what the hell use is that to you?' and she said:

'I'm glad you picked Ormeswich and not one of the other places.'

The next afternoon he saw Arlene again and came to the house again. She could tell at once that his fatal reasonableness was tempting him into compromise. No, he wasn't going to turn back, but he ought to go home and tidy things up for them. It was the least he could do.

She had no right to argue. She had no rights over him at all. His wife and two children and his business had been there long before she entered his life — or he entered hers, whichever way round it was.

'I won't be staying,' he said. 'It's only to sort things out and then leave them to it.'

She could only nod. No right to make conditions or ask for reassurances.

Again as they talked there was Peter in the next room, and again Major Kendrick upstairs. Peter would still be there and the major would still be there upstairs when there was no longer any Harry.

That made her dizzy again, and sick inside.

The words ran out. They had said all they could say. They sat at the piano and played, and at last Harry left to find Arlene and settle what time they would set out for Helming Hill.

'If I go back . . . just for a little while.'

She had stood at this window and watched him go. It had been dark then. It was daylight now; but the inner darkness was worse, if anything.

The girl was late for her lesson. Looking along the deserted street, Judith realised that she wouldn't be coming.

That made the third one already.

When the hour was up she set out to meet Harry. She wasn't confident that he would be there. The funeral had been yesterday. There must have been things to keep him there; nothing to bring him back here.

They had agreed on a stretch of the shore ten minutes north of the town. A shallow cliff dipped through a threadbare plantation of Scots pine to oil-flecked sand. Some of the oil driven in by the current had coagulated into half a dozen evilly glossy tumuli. No road came anywhere near, and even in summer few visitors came this far. In winter the shore was untrodden for a month or more at a time.

Harry was there, waiting. They kissed.

He said: 'Anything happen while I was away?'

She told him about the questions she had been asked this morning. 'But they can't go on thinking it's you,' she said, 'unless they think I'm a liar, and the major's senile.'

'Which they're capable of doing.' He put his arm round her. She buried her face in his shoulder; 'And honestly, who else could it be but me?' She shook her head, burrowed deeper to shut out the world. He said: 'You know it wasn't me, don't you?'

She freed herself and looked at him. 'I have to know that, don't I?'

'Because you know what time I left, that afternoon, and the time they say she — '

'No,' said Judith. 'I'm not doing sums. I just have to believe. Just like that. Because.'

A timber boat was anchored in the lee of the promontory. It was raining out there. Riding lights blinked through a murk of windblown drizzle.

Harry said: 'Now you're mixed up in it, too, and I've made a worse mess than before.'

Suddenly it was too much. She burst out: 'Why do you have to keep grabbing the blame for things? You're so . . . so arrogant.'

'Arrogant?' He was taken aback.

'You don't call it humility, do you, wanting to shoulder responsibility for everyone who comes anywhere near you? Because your wife wasn't fit to live with.'

'I never said anything to you about — '

'No. The perfect gentleman, accepting all the blame. But if she was even halfway all right, would you have gone out that night to kill yourself? And that brother of hers . . . all right, you didn't say anything about him, not in so many words, but even when you put it politely you made it stink.'

'I shouldn't have done that. I didn't mean to.'

'Anything else you didn't mean to do?'

He smiled wryly, with a terrible tiredness. 'Since you ask . . . '

'Tell me the worst.'

'Veronica. Norman's wife. I wrote to her — when I thought it'd be the last letter I should ever write — and it looks as though I did a lot of damage.'

'You're dangerous, aren't you?' She tried to laugh. It wouldn't come. 'You haven't told me about Veronica before.'

He told her. She listened, but couldn't visualise the woman. None of it was real. These other people didn't exist for her. But they existed for Harry.

When he had finished, she blazed: 'You

see! You're at it again! Did you drive your brother-in-law's wife to drink in the first place?'

'No, but — '

'Just saying it, you see how silly it is. So complicated, heaven knows how many removes. Try it out: your brother-in-law's wife. Drinking herself into a stupor over the years, and just because she or her husband — her full-time husband, who's had every chance of tidying up the mess for himself if he'd wanted to — because she misinterprets a friendly word from you, or a letter, or because *he* misinterprets it, you reach for the sackcloth and ashes. Maybe if you went back far enough you'd find she never stood a chance anyway: it may all have started with her mum and dad, warping her before her husband ever got near her. And then him and his sister — a right fine pair, and you still feel guilty. Did they ever feel guilty?'

'That's not the point. The fact that they could do things — shabby things — without worrying didn't mean that I — '

'Arrogant!' she said again. 'You mean

you're so much more intelligent than they are? Because you're so superior, it's your personal fault if anything goes wrong. Never theirs.'

'Judith,' he said, bewildered.

'Don't you ever wonder how far back you'd have to go to find the real person to blame? To blame for anything or anybody? Maybe if some man hadn't crossed the road two hundred years ago he wouldn't have met the girl he decided to marry, and their children and grandchildren wouldn't have existed, and there wouldn't have been any Arlene and Norman. Or if there'd been a sort of halfway Arlene and Norman, they'd have been quite different. And who says it's your inescapable burden to shove them on to the path of righteousness? Or to be responsible for anyone else? If they choose to misinterpret you, or rely on you more than you want to be relied on, that's their own lookout, not yours. And take me. *Me*. If my husband had still been alive, you'd never have met me. I wouldn't have been on that promenade at that particular moment, and those yobs wouldn't have been there, or if they had we wouldn't have met anyway — and what about responsibility for *their* existence and the way they use it? — and you wouldn't have met me.'

'Adding it all up, you'd have been a lot better off.'

'I've told you, I don't go in for doing sums.' She was cold, her breasts were aching; she was racked by love and fury. 'You're too keen on lists. You want everything tabulated. In your tidy little notebook it probably shows under the debits that you seduced me.'

'I — '

'You didn't,' she cried. 'You didn't. I wanted you. D'you hear? I *wanted* you. And I still do.'

'I don't know,' he said, choked, 'what I've done to deserve it.'

'You don't deserve things,' said Judith. 'Nobody does. They just happen.'

* * *

Peter came out of school with his collar more crumpled even than usual. There was a smear of dirt under one eye. He might have been crying; or been close to it.

They crossed the churchyard. Wrecking activities were still suspended.

Peter said: 'Mum, is it true that Uncle Harry — '

'Whatever they say about him, it's not true.'

'No.' He put his hand in hers. 'I knew it wasn't.'

She was tempted to go down the steps and along the promenade, where they wouldn't see a soul if they were lucky. Instead, she gripped Peter's hand and they walked slowly and steadily through the town. She saw a head bob up above the display in the chemist's window; and two heads came gloatingly together in a doorway.

A mother with a boy of Peter's age crossed the road to avoid speaking to her.

'This town,' she said very quietly, like a subdued curse.

Her eyes pricked. She wasn't going to cry, not out here where they could all see. Mustn't.

Church and street and shops, the sky and the gruffly breathing sea — all were just the same as ever. But she would never again be happy in Ormeswich.

10

The meeting was held in the British Legion hall, hired for the occasion.

Sherwill was there early, setting up a table inside the doors and stacking the forms they had prepared for signature after the speakers had put their case. He looked startled when he saw Harold.

'Didn't think you'd show up.'

'After all the work we've put into it, I want to see the pay-off. Think people are going to turn up?'

'I'm sure they are.'

Sherwill watched unhappily as Harold went into the hall. Two tables had been pushed together on the platform, with five seats behind and one seat at each end. Harold did a quick count in his head. Including himself, there ought to be eight people on the platform.

Tucker came in behind him.

'Oh, Pearson. I mean . . . Grant.'

'I gather we're hoping for a full house.'

'Well, yes. Hoping, naturally.' Tucker sagged, his head bobbed as he appeared to count the rows of folding chairs. 'Are you really up to it?' he asked. 'I mean, this upsetting business you've gone through . . . '

'You mean you'd sooner I took a back seat?'

'My dear chap, it's entirely up to you. You've done so much. If you want to take it easy, no one'll blame you.'

'Or no seat at all?' said Harold.

'Tell you what. Why don't you hold what they call a watching brief? As a stranger you'll be able to see it a lot more clearly than the rest of us. I mean, this is basically an Ormeswich matter. Better leave this public bit of it to Ormeswich. Then see how we go.'

'Yes, let's see how we go,' said Harold. And went.

He was glad of Ormeswich's inadequate street lighting. Not that there were many people about. Most of them would be watching a quiz programme on the box; the more active ones would be getting ready to go to the meeting.

He dawdled close to the door of a pub, then passed it. He had been a fool to think, lulled by the make-believe weeks in a make-believe town, that the place had any intention of offering anything to an alien like himself.

Harold, I want you to come home. I mean it. I didn't know you'd felt so badly about everything. I never thought of you doing anything like this. Maybe it's been a lesson. For both of us. We can be mature about it. If you'll come back and talk it all over . . .

A splash of light spilled into the street from the garage on the corner. A shiny new van had turned out of one of the lock-ups but was blocked by the firm's breakdown truck. The manager stood by one of the petrol pumps, his hands spread apologetically.

'It's not up to me, Sid. Honest. If it was just me, all right. You know me. But the finance company are on my back.'

Harold went on. If he stayed here, perhaps there would be openings for him. Garages were always in trouble over repair bills, over quick sales and slow payments. And in a place run the way Ormeswich was run there were plenty of shopkeepers and tradesmen who could use the services of an expert debt collector.

He shuddered at the prospect.

But what else?

I don't see why it would have to be the same as it was before. Why shouldn't we change it? Harold, you don't have to look at me like that. You don't have to hate me. What are you going to do, then — just quit again, leave us all in a mess, not knowing . . . ?

Between two houses he glimpsed the lighthouse. Its lantern was a shadowy silhouette against the sky; then the glowing, sparking heart of a Catherine wheel, flailing its beam against a row of chimneys and then out over the waves. The church tower loomed stark and solid, then was blanked out; solidified again, disappeared again. The light went out.

Harold skirted the silent churchyard. Light splashed into it, was sucked away, came round again.

Lucky old Angus McMenemy.

He made another circuit of the town and was drawn inevitably to the undistinguished street that had become the most important street in Ormeswich to him.

The light was on in the front window, the curtains drawn. He remembered approaching the house a few weeks ago, a lifetime ago, and hearing a Bach toccata spraying its limpid notes jubilantly out from that room. There was no sound now.

He went up to the door and rang the bell.

Judith stood in the doorway, holding the door only partially open, as though not sure who to expect.

So it's your piano teacher. Oh, yes, I've heard about her. Didn't waste any time, did you? Footy-footy on the pedals — makes you feel young again?

Peter came curiously out of the room at the back, holding a comic. He hesitated, then said bravely: 'Hello, Uncle Harry.' He came along the passage, gripped Harold's arm for a moment, then went back.

Judith said: 'Not at the meeting?'

'It was hinted that my presence could be dispensed with.'

She led the way into the front room. 'Yes, I had an idea something like that might be said.' She slammed down the lid of the piano keyboard. Harmonics jangled faintly from inside. She said: 'Major Kendrick's gone.'

'He'd be there early, on the platform.'

'No, I mean he's gone for good.'

'Slunk off?' Harold felt winded. 'I'd never have thought it of him.'

'I asked him to go.'

'You — '

'I told him I didn't know what my future plans were. I might have to move, sell the house — I didn't know. It would be a good thing if he found somewhere else.'

'I'm glad he didn't leave off his own bat.'

'He'd have stuck it out. But he was awfully relieved when I made it easy for him. It was no use, you know: we couldn't talk any more, even saying good morning was an ordeal.'

'It's ridiculous,' he exploded. 'Absolutely monstrous, all of it.'

She took an envelope off the top of the piano and handed it to him. He unfolded the headed sheet of letter paper inside. It was from the private school where she taught music once a week. Because of a change of curriculum, coming into force immediately, Mrs. Marshall's services would no longer be required. The headmistress thanked her for all the help she had given in the past. A cheque was enclosed.

'At least there was a cheque,' said Judith. 'The others . . . '

'What others?'

Half her pupils had dropped off. Only two parents had written notes to tell her about the withdrawal; and only one had so far paid.

They sat on the couch, simply holding hands. At one stage he put his arm round her and drew her close, but she began to cry, without tears.

The piano remained closed. They didn't dare touch it. He sensed her unspoken fear that the neighbours, who had never complained before, would now seize the excuse to start banging on the wall.

When he walked back to the smoke-house, along the promenade, it was nearly high tide. The roar of the sea was a crude anaesthetic.

Through it he could still hear that voice.

And you did write to Veronica, didn't you? As well as those beastly, double-crossing things you sent to me and Norman. After all we'd done for you. Honestly, Harold, I never knew you had it in you. Drooling over the poor creature like that, and then leaving her to the bottle — and not even going through with your sick romantic flourish in the end.

The window of the smokehouse was patterned with odd reflections and dull non-reflections as he crunched round it to the door. The glass had been smashed. Inside, two large pebbles lay on the faded rug. The wind carried a fine spray in through the jagged holes.

And what will your pretty little pianist do when you wander off again? Because I suppose that's what you'll be doing. Another maudlin letter — and where will you go next time?

He went out with the torch, which the owners had left above the fireplace, and found some torn planks and boxes in the dunes. He wedged bits and pieces as well as he could into the window frame, and went to bed.

It was not Arlene's voice he heard now as he lay awake, but his own. Not as querulous as Arlene's but asking questions, like hers, that couldn't be answered. Couldn't be but had to be. Staying in Ormeswich or leaving, what was he going to do? Judith had always said she couldn't think of going away; for himself, how could he possibly stay? And to start again — to launch out, saying it was a fresh start . . . he knew there was no such thing. Knew it all too well, now. It was a world of formalised salaries and pensions, of insurance cards, accountants and tax men with tabs on you, of forms in quadruplicate and questionnaires which had to be filled in accurately if you wished to be allowed to go on breathing. And policemen with unfinished business, still watching and speculating.

You could choose to finish it; but not to restart.

In the morning, just before lunchtime, when he knew the bar would be open, he walked into the Godyll Club.

Sir Douglas Mallard was the first to spot him. He got out of his chair muttering, as if to block the invasion.

Tucker, at the bar, turned in dismay.

Harold said: 'Won't keep you a minute. 1 just dropped in to give you my resignation from the action committee.'

'Oh.' The wind was taken out of Tucker's sails. 'Well, of course. Needn't have bothered, though: I mean, no need for formalities. We'd have got the message.'

Harold held out the bulky envelope. 'And I've attached my working notes. They may come in handy.'

'This is all very well,' Mallard barked.

'How did it go last night?' Harold asked.

'Stopped them in their tracks, by the look of it.' Tucker allowed a touch of affability now that the threatening embarrassment had been written off. 'They'll have to replant the shrubs, and apply through the proper channels for a Faculty. Sherwill took the forms and our surveyor's report to the town hall this morning. They'll be a bit more careful now. Probably consult us before trying anything else. Otherwise we'll appeal against the Faculty.'

'Splendid.'

'Well . . . ' They were waiting for Harold to go. 'Good of you to bring this . . . er . . . this guff. Most useful.'

'I'll be off,' said Harold. 'Couldn't ever become a member of the Club now,' he added, and heard Mallard snort indignantly. 'I'm going into trade, and you don't allow those sort of people, do you?'

'In trade?' said Tucker. 'Here?'

'Could be.'

He turned away. They were dying to know. At the door, he said:

'You may have heard of Pledge and Distraint Services. Or you may not. The old family firm. Haven't reached here yet, but it's time we did: time we expanded into the provinces. Bad debts grow just as luxuriantly here as in London.'

'Debt collecting?' said Mallard, disgusted.

'I imagine you wouldn't approve, Sir Douglas.'

'I suppose some people will do anything to scratch a living.'

'The scratchings add up. Small debts, but they all add up. Riding fees, piano lessons, garage bills — I'll be demonstrating the technique very shortly. Quite a burst of publicity, you'll see.'

He left.

Two days later Judith received a cheque for the amount outstanding on piano lessons for the Mallards' daughter.

It was on the same day that Harold got a note slipped through the smokehouse door from the estate agents, regretting that in view of damage which had occurred during his tenancy, which was contrary to the terms of the tenancy, he must be asked to vacate the premises by the end of the week. Their clients had authorised the refund of the money for the remaining period, less the cost of essential repairs.

'I could fight it, of course,' he said.

'I don't think I can fight,' said Judith. 'I don't think I can go on living here.'

If only they could find Arlene's killer. But they were trying in one direction only. Because he was the likeliest candidate. There wasn't anybody else. And the police couldn't be expected to know that there *had* to be somebody else. Because he hadn't killed Arlene.

So the unsolved mystery would haunt

him for the rest of his life?

He said: 'I'll go and see Norman. Fight something out with him.'

'Going back? But you couldn't bear it.'

'That set-up needs straightening out. I let things slide too easily, in the past — let him have his own way instead of sticking to what I knew could be done. Now we'll see. There are other ways of doing things.'

'I won't have it. I won't have you, just because of me — '

'Now *you're* at it!' He tried to wring a smile from her. 'The other day you were blaming me for shouldering responsibility for other people and what they did. Now you're doing it yourself.'

'You hate the idea of going back,' she said, 'even for a day. I know you do.'

He said: 'I don't know what else there is to do.'

*   *   *

For some reason the garage could not supply a car and driver to take him the fifteen miles to the station. He had to wait for the bus, which would take forty-five minutes to do the journey.

As he stood at the stop, Mrs. Ainsworth passed, slow and erect. Then she looked back at him, did a military about-turn, and tapped her cane along the pavement towards him.

'You're that young man who's been trying to stop them digging up our graves, aren't you?' Her face was seamed like a walnut. Her eyes were glittering black beads. She said: 'Nothing I wanted to be bothered with. Not for a start. But now, you want me to sign, I'll sign.'

'Thank you, Mrs. Ainsworth. I'm not on the committee any more, though.'

'The town clerk,' she said. 'Now, who'd 'a thought it? Comes round and says if I'll speak up for their lot, he won't move none of our family stones. He'll see to it, he says.' She waited for a shocked response. 'One of them Palmers,' she said scornfully. 'Never been any quality, them Palmers. Trying to bribe *me*! So if you want me to say so, I reckon I'm on your side.'

The bus came in from the end of the High Street, backed down the entrance to

Peddars Place, and swung towards the bus stop.

Harold said: 'Mrs. Ainsworth, I think things were cleared up pretty well at the meeting last night.'

'Last night?' She shook her head.

'If you'd care to approach Mr. Tucker,' he said, 'or Major Kendrick . . . '

She watched, disappointed, as he got on the bus. She obviously thought he was impatient to be rid of her.

It had taken a long time for the churchyard controversy to impinge on her. He wondered how long it would take her to learn of the inquest on Mrs. Harold Grant, and to register that he was the Harold Grant who ought never to have come to this town in the first place.

11

The new recruit looked pleased, though a bit uncertain of what he'd got to be pleased about.

'Good work, lad.' Norman flicked the signed form with his fingernail.

'It's not much of a haul, sir. I mean, fifty pence a week when possible until the debts cleared — it's going to take a long while to pay off.'

Norman shook his head. 'You still don't get it? What counts is that this slippery customer has been denying all along that he did owe the money. Now he's signed agreeing that he does — and thinking we're letting him off lightly — we've got him. The hell with fifty pence a week 'when possible': he's acknowledged liability, and we take him straight to court for the whole lot.'

The phone rang. Mrs. Barsham murmured into it, then tilted the receiver meaningfully towards him. Norman nodded an affable dismissal to the young man, and said:

'Yes? Leggett here.'

'It's Harold.'

'Oh. It is, is it? And where are you this time?'

'Liverpool Street. I want to talk to you.'

Norman looked at Mrs. Barsham. She was studying the red drawing pins dotting the wall map.

'Come to my place — about six. That suit you?'

'Not the office?' said Harold. 'This is business.'

'We can talk more easily at home,' said Norman.

He found it hard to concentrate for the rest of the afternoon. Business, Harold had said: what kind of business? Nothing personal — no theories about what had happened, no theories springing out of that one thing which Harold knew for certain?

Norman thrust it to the back of his mind, where it had been kept well muzzled ever since the blow fell.

Harold arrived at the house ten

minutes after Norman had poured himself a large whisky.

'Now, what's it all about?' He decided to strike an amiable note at the beginning. If there had to be a row later, he'd be the one to decide when, and how far to go.

Harold said: 'I've been thinking of coming back into the firm.'

'You have?' Not so good.

'But I don't think it would work.'

Better. 'Certainly wouldn't do our public image any good,' said Norman.

'So I'm looking for a deal that'll set me up somewhere, on my own, well away from here.'

'Ormeswich, for instance?'

'I think that's ruled out, now.'

'I'd imagine so.' Norman felt that Harold was prowling round him in search of an undefended flank. But Harold couldn't possibly suspect. And if he did, whose fault was it, at root? He said: 'What have you got in mind?'

'I need to know how much money is available.'

'For you? Well, look . . . we don't

exactly owe you anything;'

'Don't you?'

'Harold, old son, you know we slimmed you down for the bankruptcy. There's no big share for you in the company. Wouldn't have been legal to salt anything away for you on the side,' he added virtuously.

Harold said: 'I want to call in the full sum on the house.'

'Hey, now, wait a minute there.'

'The money from the house,' said Harold. 'and a share of the firm's assets commensurate with the work I put into building it up.'

'What's all this about?'

'How much?' said Harold bluntly.

'You want to marry your piano piece?' Norman had a stab at it, and saw from Harold's face that he was right. 'Hey, it's a bit early, isn't it?'

'We're talking business, nothing else.'

'Your wife's conveniently murdered, and right away you're — '

'Conveniently?' Harold's tone was ominous. 'I didn't kill her.'

'Lots of people think you did. Including the police.'

'Because you've done your best to make them think so.'

'Me? Look,' said Norman, 'every time they've put it to me I've said it couldn't be you. And if they find out in the end it *is* you, in spite of everything I've said, then it must be because you were so disturbed you weren't responsible for your actions.'

Harold was sitting comfortably back in his chair, but there was a tautness in his arms threatening a sudden thrust forward.

Norman said placatingly: 'If I were you I'd let it rest. Give things a chance to blow over. Then if you still feel like making beautiful music with your piano teacher, well, that's up to you.'

'In the meantime,' said Harold, 'the money.'

'Any right-minded person would agree that I oughtn't to allow you unrestricted use of any substantial amount of capital.'

Outside he heard the rattle of gravel as a car slithered to a halt on the drive. It couldn't be Mrs. Barsham. Even if she had driven over in a hurry with some urgent last-minute information on something, she would never have skidded up the drive like that.

Harold was saying: 'Apparently you told the police that you and Arlene had received no final letters from me.'

'You were upset that night. You don't know whether you posted letters or — or even whether you wrote them.'

'You got them all right. And I can always rewrite them from memory if I have to — the financial details in them, anyway.'

Half listening, waiting for the doorbell, Norman was snatched back. 'What? You trying some kind of blackmail?'

'If the police get too insistent, and you keep hinting to them that I'm round the bend, I can give them enough chapter and verse to make them start wondering.'

'You twisting little bastard.'

A key grated in the lock. The front door opened.

Veronica crossed the hall and came into the sitting room. She took two steps towards Norman, then saw Harold. Before she could speak, Norman was on his feet.

'What d'you think you're doing here?'

'I discharged myself,' said Veronica in a faraway whisper, not taking her eyes off Harold.

'They had no right to let you out.'

'It's not a prison, Norman. Not quite. The inmates do have the right to walk out when they can't bear it there any longer.'

Harold stood up and held out his hand. 'Hello, Veronica.'

She was thinner than ever. Her eyes burned mauve in her drawn, bleached face. 'I've been waiting for you to come back, Harold. I was wondering how long you'd be.'

'Go and lie down. I'll ring them, find out what's been going on.' Norman took her arm, all skin and bone, brittle between his fingers but resistant. 'Come on — a rest is what you need. You promised me this time — '

'Promises.' She giggled.

'Harold' — Norman jerked a thumb at the writing table — 'there's a bottle of tablets in that drawer, the right-hand one, under the — '

'Thank you for your letter,' Veronica

said to Harold. 'Your dear, dear letter.'

He said: 'There's something I've got to say to you.'

'So much,' she murmured. 'Lots and lots, I hope.'

'That letter. I had no right to send it.'

'Shut up, for God's sake,' said Norman.

'You had every right.' Veronica stood between them, Norman vainly gripping her arm, Harold's hand softly imprisoned in hers.

'I should never have written it,' said Harold. 'It must have given you a lot of pain. I'm deeply sorry.'

'Pain?' Her marvelling eyes drooped shut, opened again in slow motion. 'Just the opposite.'

'I only wanted to wish you well,' he said.

'And you're still alive to do it.' She tugged away from Norman, closer to Harold.

Norman cracked. He had lived with it, with her in the house and then without her, while Harold's two sullen, preoccupied children came and went their own surly ways. He wanted to smash something. He had to lash out.

'Give up!' he yelled. 'Don't you know

289

when to give up?'

'I'll get those tablets,' said Harold.

'I don't need them,' said Veronica. 'I don't have to do everything Norman says. Not now you're here.'

'Look at him,' Norman raved on. 'Look at him — take a really good look! Don't you see? He's going to get married. Married!'

She nodded abstractedly. 'Such a lot to talk about.'

'He's got a nice little dolly in Ormeswich. Right, Harold? For God's sake din it into her and let's be done with it. You're going to get married, aren't you?'

'Yes.'

Veronica emerged from her abstraction. 'Oh, but you can't do that, Harold,' she said, clearly and simply. 'You know there's nobody else. There couldn't be.'

'So much for your sick daydreams,' said Norman.

It was no daydream, it was an obsession. 'Harold,' she said, 'after all I've done for you . . .'

'That's enough.' Norman tried to get a fresh grip on her. 'Come on, now. We'll sort it all out later.'

'Don't you think it's symbolic, the way I decided to come home just the day you were here? There's always been that bond between us — you can't break it. And now we've come together.' She shivered. 'That awful place — it was so cold.'

'She can't think straight.' Norman shrugged a man-to-man laugh at Harold. 'The heating in that place she goes to is like an oven.'

Harold himself looked icy cold. He said: 'Yes, it's a draughty place, Ormeswich.'

'Who's talking about Ormeswich?'

'What possessed you to go there?' asked Veronica.

'You need your gloves on all the time,' said Harold tonelessly.

'Oh, indeed you do.' She slid her hand out of his at last and turned it over, studying it. 'You do.'

Harold said, over her shoulder: 'How long have you known about this?'

'She has nightmares,' said Norman. 'All your fault.'

'You packed her off to that home the moment she got back?'

'He was jealous,' said Veronica. 'With reason,' she said archly.

Norman went to the drawer and found the tablets. She turned away and poured herself a drink, a large one. He didn't care. It had had to come to this, and now might as well play itself out. When he held two tablets towards her in his palm, she took them automatically, slipped them into her mouth, and drank

Harold said: 'Veronica. How did it happen?'

'She was sneering. Wouldn't stop. You know how she was. Cheap sneers, all about you, all set to ruin it all for you again, the way she'd been doing it all those years. She went striding along, and I had to run to keep up with her, and she sneered at me . . . but it was worst about you . . . and I couldn't stand it. So I hit her.' Veronica held out her empty glass for more. 'And she went over. And I drove home to wait for you.'

'But . . .'

'Don't ask the whys and wherefores,' said Norman, tired beyond endurance. 'She doesn't think things through, the

292

way the rest of us have to.'

Veronica was relaxing. She yawned, apologised with a demure little smile, sat down, and stared fondly at Harold.

He said: 'How did you know where Arlene would be?'

'I hung about and waited for her,' said Veronica inconsequentially.

Norman said: 'Snooping, as usual. Listening on the extension the night Arlene rang me from Ormeswich. And driving off next day, just like that. You see?' It was harsh and sour in his throat. 'You do see, now, what you started?'

'Yes,' said Veronica. 'You do see you couldn't think of marrying this woman, whoever she is — if Norman hasn't just made her up.'

'He hasn't made her up,' said Harold.

She shook her head, dismissing the very idea of it. She seemed content now. When Norman helped her to her feet she offered no resistance. He took her upstairs and waited until she was stretched out, fully clothed, on the bed. She mumbled something to herself — a drowsy, satisfied sound.

He went back to the sitting room.

Harold's hands were shaking. Norman was glad. It was high time Harold suffered.

He said: 'So now you know.'

'Tell me one thing.' Harold tried to steady himself, tried to reason things out where there was nothing that was reasonable. 'Did you seriously think you could pin that murder on me — get me out of the way, let me carry the can?'

Norman said frankly: 'I don't know what I thought. I didn't know which way to play it. And hell, you didn't do it — not with your own hands, so they could never really have got you for it — but if it hadn't been for you, it would never have happened. So why shouldn't you sweat?'

'You think Veronica would have kept quiet while they brought me to trial? Sentenced me, even.'

'It wouldn't ever have come to that. How could it? It would all have fizzled out. It all *will* fizzle out.'

'And then?'

'Maybe you were right,' said Norman. 'About coming back.'

Harold didn't understand.

'Into the firm.' Norman warmed to it. 'Maybe it's best, after all. Keep the whole thing between us.'

'The whole thing? Including Veronica?'

Between us, thought Norman. Yes, this had to be it. If Harold was what she wanted, it would take the load off his own back. Harold had got them this far: let him cope from now on. She'd always had this thing about him. Let him cope, instead of running off. It was neat. Less trouble than anything else would be.

He said: 'Don't you think you owe her something? You're the only one who can keep things all right for her.'

Harold doubled up with an inner spasm, his hand across his eyes. 'All right . . . for her?' The questioning echo was barely audible.

'I'll tell you one thing.' Norman could restrain it no longer. 'That night when you walked out — it's a pity you didn't make a proper job of it.'

12

The coroner read the two letters that Harold Grant had written, the first to his brother-in-law and one-time partner, and the second to Mrs. Judith Marshall. They were short and explicit. They expressed regret for the distress he had caused in the past and the unhappiness he might now cause, but left no doubt that he had set out on the stormy night of Tuesday the 7th of March with the intention of putting an end to his life.

A fisherman who had reported his long-shore boat missing on the morning of the 8th, presumably carried off by the high seas, which had scoured shore and harbour all night, reclaimed the boat when it was washed ashore, upside-down, on the Norfolk coat near Bacton. A waterlogged jacket identified as belonging to Harold Grant was caught up between two loose planks of the inboard engine housing. A shoe which could not have been in the water much longer than a couple of days was later found on the shore two miles north of Ormeswich, and was identified by a local shopkeeper as probably one of a pair which he had sold to Mr. Grant a week ago.

The coroner heard evidence from Mr. Norman Leggett that his brother-in-law had contemplated suicide shortly before coming to Ormeswich, and Chedstowe C.I.D. reported a recent statement made to them by Mr. Grant himself confirming that this had been his intention. The police had in fact confiscated the gun with which he had originally meant to take his life, and had been about to initiate proceedings against Mr. Grant for possessing a firearm without a firearm certificate.

The coroner was by training reluctant to presume death without the existence of a corpse, but there was no guarantee that this would ever be washed up on the coast. Too many local men had been lost at sea, at one time and another, for him to feel justified in postponing a verdict.

The authenticity of the letters was in

no doubt. The long-shore boat had clearly been taken out to sea on a night when no experienced fisherman would have gone out. Whether Harold Grant had merely gone far enough out to throw himself overboard, or whether at the last minute he had wanted to return but been washed over as the boat capsized, it was impossible to tell, and hardly relevant. The balance of probabilities was on the side of his having committed suicide. This verdict was duly recorded.

Mr. Wratten's duties were not yet at an end. Ormeswich had never known so many inquisitions in such a short space of time. After a tactful interval, which deceived nobody, he resumed the inquest on Mrs. Harold Grant. The detective-inspector in charge of the police investigation testified that, although an absolutely conclusive charge could not have been brought, he and his colleagues were confident that their inquiries had been rightly narrowed down to one particular person. These inquiries could not be completed to their entire satisfaction because the person had since died.

It was the coroner's decision, in line

with current rulings on the subject, that no public good would be served by naming the suspect.

A verdict was recorded of murder by the hand of someone known but unnamed.

★   ★   ★

Norman Leggett assumed that he had seen and heard the last of Ormeswich. He was wrong. After Harold's will was proven, he found it imperative to visit the town again.

Harold had made a new will three days before deciding to drown himself. It had been drawn up by a Chedstowe solicitor, and named Major Kendrick as executor. It left Harold's remaining worldly goods divided into two equal parts: one part to be shared between his son and daughter, the other half for Mrs. Judith Marshall.

The executor had applied to call in the full sum, which Mr. Norman Leggett owed the late Mr. Harold Grant on the house sold to him by Mr. Grant. He also asked for a statement of any pension, life insurance and like monies payable to Mr.

Grant's estate, and for a statement of any sums outstanding from his late wife's estate.

Norman gathered that Major Kendrick had been reluctant to accept the chore of executor; but with Mrs. Marshall's welfare at heart he was bent on seeing everything done in good order.

Certainly the will was in good order: technically it was unimpeachable.

Harold had been quite clear about what to do and who to choose.

Norman sat a few feet from the piano, thought incongruously of Harold sitting there playing his scales or five-finger exercises or whatever, and said:

'I'm so glad you could manage to see me, Mrs. Marshall. It's a bit of a tricky situation.'

The soft approach, as usual. The usual timing.

'I thought it was all very clear,' she said.

'Harold's death came as a great shock to us.'

'Although you knew he'd been driven close to it once before?'

Judith Marshall wasn't at all what he had expected. A piano teacher, Sandy had said over the phone; and he could still hear Arlene saying it scornfully, and see what she visualized — some frumpish middle-aged spinster or a gawky young woman giving lessons at home because she had an ageing mother to look after, or just wasn't good enough at anything else. With glasses. He didn't know why, but glasses were an inevitable part of the outfit. And here she was, the real Mrs. Marshall.

She was sure of herself, in a way he couldn't define. Sure of what she was sure of. Not obstinate or insular or straight-laced, but sturdy.

He wouldn't have minded catching her off balance, with a few debts showing. Get her down, put her through it. Though he had an uncomfortable feeling she wasn't the type.

She'd been the type for Harold, hadn't she? Or hadn't she — had it been just another of those airy-fairy things like the one he'd got Veronica into?

Mrs. Marshall didn't fit there, either.

He said: 'It's a delicate matter. There are the children to think of. Harold's children.'

'He thought of them.' She was matter-of-fact without sounding callous.

'He adored those kids. When he was really himself, he adored them.'

'Did he?'

'Mrs. Marshall. Or look, couldn't I call you Judith?' It was time for the warm-up. Tackle it as a routine job and it would work out the way routine jobs always worked when he really got cracking. 'Somehow I feel I've known you a long time. Funny how it sometimes happens, isn't it?'

'Harry told me a lot about you,' she said.

'You and he were very close. I know that. And he and I worked very closely for a long, long time.'

'He told me,' she said.

Her tone sounded far from promising.

'Absolutely frank with each other, right? Put all our cards on the table.' Norman's hands sketched an outgoing parabola from chest level. It was one of the first things they had taught the paw-flappers on their executive courses. Nowadays there was hardly a television interviewer who didn't use the rhythmic, bountiful gesture. 'Do you think maybe your friend, Kendrick — chap Harold chose to look after your interests — maybe he's being a bit hasty?'

'Major Kendrick's not what I'd call a hasty person.'

'Calling in all the money like that, all at once. On the house, I mean.'

'Can't you afford it, Mr. Leggett?'

'Norman,' he said. 'Norman, right?' When she said nothing, he went on: 'It's just that I didn't bank on it being called in. That wasn't the arrangement we made.'

'We?'

'Harold and I,' he said. 'It was all a legal thing, you know. Tax and so on.'

'I'm not very good at that sort of thing,' she said. 'I've never had that much money to play around with.'

'No.' He seized on this. 'Having a hunk of capital dumped in your lap when you're not used to handling the stuff can be more trouble than it's worth. What you need is steady comfort, right? Look,

Judith, why don't we leave the situation the way it is for the time being? I'm sure Kendrick'll take your instructions if you tell him that that's what you want. I go on paying you interest, the way I paid Harold — maybe a lower rate, because it was rather a special family deal I had with Harold, and — '

'Harry left it in his will that I was to have the money now,' she said calmly.

'You really want it that badly?'

'It's what Harry wanted.'

'You must have had quite some influence over him.'

A duster of freckles above her cheekbones deepened in colour. Her voice remained steady. 'Did you come all the way to Ormeswich just to find out how much?'

'There's another aspect of it.'

'Yes?'

'The kids,' he said. 'Nigel and Amanda. Nigel's school fees are pretty steep, and there'll be more to pay out later. And Amanda's going to need a lot this next year or two. Do you genuinely think you ought to take that full half? I mean, even a three-way split, with a third each for the children and you . . . maybe some small allowance for me, to help with their expenses . . . '

'If Harry had wanted to leave you anything,' she said, 'I think he'd have put it in the will.'

There was nothing overtly hostile in her manner. She was simply, drily stating what she felt.

'If we chose to contest it — '

'On what grounds?'

'Look, it sticks out a mile he was upset. He went out and killed himself afterwards, didn't he?'

'If you're going to try that old 'while the balance of his mind was disturbed' business, I don't think the solicitor and Major Kendrick would support it. Try it, Mr. Leggett, and you'll find the larger share of the money will end up in lawyers' pockets. That much I do know.'

He saw with stony certainty that he was going to get nowhere. He didn't stand a chance.

As though she knew he had surrendered, she said pleasantly: 'Mr. Leggett, I didn't really want this money. When I first heard about it I nearly got in touch with you.'

'Well, I'm here now.'

'And now I've met you,' she said, 'I see that Major Kendrick's right. It *is* what Harry wanted.'

The loving curve of her lips was too much for him. 'What Harry wanted! All that wet sentimentality, all the . . . the trouble that man caused . . . '

'Oh, trouble, yes,' she said. 'But he was so cuddly.'

'Cuddly?' Norman was stunned. 'I've never heard anyone call him that before.'

'More fool them,' said Judith Marshall. And, sadly: 'More fool *her*.'

★   ★   ★

Spring was turning to an early summer in Porthmullin. The window of the *Golden Hind* was open on to the warm breeze from the cove. Muffled by the sleepy lapping of the water on the hard, a steady tapping and sawing came from the boatyard. There were four men at the bar, two lounging in the window seat, and one standing by the fireplace.

'Got round to putting us in a book yet, Crispian?'

'You mean is he getting ready to cash in and then make a run for it?'

'Writin' a dirty novel about you, Ben — that what you scared of?'

It was a regular midday exchange. The pub, like so many along this stretch of the Cornish coast, had its tame painter, a potter, one lady weaver, and an author, to leaven the dour, slow-spoken fishermen and the noisy sailing fraternity. Crispian Higgins had been here long enough to have his appointed place at the bar.

Henry Marshall had been here long enough to be welcomed by the regulars when he came into the bar, but not to have become an integral part of any group. He tended to stand at one end of the fireplace, looking out across the cove at the heaped cloud formations.

This morning Crispian brought him into the conversation. 'They're such a parochial lot here, don't you find? Believing their little intrigues can be blown up to best-sellerdom.'

The others grunted mock menace.

'And what are you actually writing at the moment?' asked Henry Marshall.

Crispian picked up his pint and moved across to the other side of the fireplace. He tried to sound casual, shrugging off the idea that anything he wrote could possibly interest anyone else; but was delighted with the opportunity.

'Husband and wife mysteries. You know, Julia Wallace in Liverpool, Adelaide Bartlett — oh, I know they've been gone over before, but there are still new theories to be explored.'

'A lot depends on the writing.'

'I do my humble best.' Crispian looked down into his beer. 'Now, what I'm particularly keen on is a recent addition. May become a classic in its time. I wouldn't mind being the first to spot its potential. I thought of it the other day when you came in.'

'Me?'

'Marshall the Mystery,' said the landlord. It was the sort of meaningless ribbing that could go on indefinitely, passing a morning or evening away.

Crispian said: 'I'm always collecting snippets from the papers. Little fag-ends of situations, ideas, you know. Anything with a bit of mystery about it. There was this report, a few months ago, about a chap called Grant who walked out on his wife — '

'Nothing mysterious about that,' chipped in a voice from the window seat. 'Only mystery is why more of us don't do it.'

'He intended to commit suicide. Or that was the story. Then showed up in a little place on the east coast under an assumed name. Pearson, I think it was. Now, for a start, why Pearson?'

'Picked it at random from a shop front,' hazarded Marshall.

'You think so? It's not impossible. But I'd be inclined to go for something deeper — something psychological.'

'Makes the book longer,' Marshall agreed.

'I've no intention of padding. But I'm sure there's a lot there anyway. You see, this Grant bloke did it again — disappeared. This time the coroner said he'd definitely committed suicide: drowned himself.'

'Often felt like that myself.' The landlord said it loudly enough for his wife to call back through the kitchen hatch: 'What are you lot on about in there?'

'Still haven't heard where Henry comes into it,' said one of the men at the bar.

Crispian said: 'It was just his name that reminded me. There was a woman called Marshall involved. I don't know how deeply involved, but she was one of those who got a suicide letter — one of the two mentioned at the inquest. Why *her*? Had he known her before, and left his wife to go and live with her? And if so, why did he quit again? I've been following it up . . . and you know what?'

'No,' said Henry Marshall. 'What?'

'He left her half his money. Now, suppose it's all a plant. Suppose he didn't do himself in, but got over to Holland or Belgium or somewhere, and he's setting up there and waiting for her to join him.' Crispian took a crumpled wad of press cuttings from an inner pocket. He unfolded three or four. 'Oh, that's the kinky one about the wife who let her husband mess about with leather belts and . . . no, not this one . . . here we are.' He held out an advertisement. From *The Times*. It's been in twice a week for the last three weeks.'

Marshall read it. He studied it for quite a time, which wasn't really necessary. It was a very short ad.

It read:

H. Sure you are there somewhere. If you need your money, please send for it. J.

'You think this has some connection?' Slowly he handed the clipping back.

'Can't be sure. But it ties in neatly, doesn't it?'

'What are you going to do, then?'

'Oh, I don't know. Dabble with the idea a bit. If I really get down to it, maybe I can trace the person who put that ad in, and if it is the Marshall woman . . . ' Crispian raised his shoulders and his eyebrows simultaneously.

Henry Marshall offered him a pint, stayed another ten minutes, and then walked up the cobbled street past the post office. He stayed at the top of the slope for a few minutes, then turned hesitantly back towards the post office.

Already he had done a little time and motion study on the boatyard where he did part-time book-keeping, and his recommendations had been accepted. He had been asked to join a committee to oppose the building of a yacht marina in the nicest part of the cove. And he was tempted to offer Crispian Higgins advice on his proposed book — more advice than it was safe for him to give.

Tempted . . . On his own he wouldn't be strong enough to resist. Already he could feel himself being drawn into the little local community.

He went into the post office and bought a letter card. At the head of it he wrote the name of Henry Marshall and his address. Then he said:

My dearest,
    I don't need the money. I need your help. I need *you*.
      Your loving
      Henry

At the last moment he almost snatched it back from the maw of the letterbox. Then it slipped through his fingers and fell in; and he heard the decisive plop as it reached the bottom.

THE END

We do hope that you have enjoyed reading this large print book.

Did you know that all of our titles are available for purchase?

We publish a wide range of high quality large print books including:
Romances, Mysteries, Classics
General Fiction
Non Fiction and Westerns

Special interest titles available in large print are:
The Little Oxford Dictionary
Music Book, Song Book
Hymn Book, Service Book

Also available from us courtesy of Oxford University Press:
Young Readers' Dictionary
(large print edition)
Young Readers' Thesaurus
(large print edition)

For further information or a free brochure, please contact us at:
Ulverscroft Large Print Books Ltd.,
The Green, Bradgate Road, Anstey,
Leicester, LE7 7FU, England.
Tel: (00 44) **0116 236 4325**
Fax: (00 44) **0116 234 0205**

Other titles in the
Linford Mystery Library:

DEATH IN THE SQUARE

Ardath Mayhar

The upper-class inhabitants of the locked-gate community called Holroyd Square in Templeton, Texas are used to their sedate, private lives — and the equally private dark secrets that each of them keeps hidden from the others. But when a vicious blackmailer rudely interrupts their existence, and is then found murdered in the Square, the police must be called. Now only Assistant Chief Wash Shipp can uncover the killer and save their tattered reputations . . .

THE SECRET ENEMY

Manning K. Robertson

It is the height of the Cold War. British Agent Steve Carradine's mission is to locate and smuggle to the West a defecting Russian scientist with the vital secret of a new technology — but the Soviets are hot on his trail. Aided by a mysterious female agent, Carradine finds Professor Ubyenkov, and the three fugitives make a desperate flight on the Orient Express in a superhuman effort to remain alive and escape to Britain.

MURDER ON ICE

Paula Williams

After her boyfriend runs out on her with the contents of their joint bank account, Kat Latcham has no choice but to return to the tiny village of Millford Magna where she grew up. The place, she complains, is not so much sleepy as comatose, and she longs for something exciting to happen. But when she and her childhood friend Will discover a body, and Will's father is suspected of murder, Kat suddenly realises she should have heeded the saying, 'Be careful what you wish for'.

MR. WHIPPLE EXPLAINS

Gerald Verner

Mr. Augustus Whipple spends most of his time reading detective stories and thrillers. And his hobby stands him in good stead when he is faced with crimes in real life, for his fictional experiences enable him to find a solution to two mysterious murders, which comes as a surprise to the police and his next door neighbour, Inspector Gallers of Scotland Yard. And Gallers has particular reason to be grateful for Mr. Whipple's hobby when he finds himself arrested as chief suspect for the second murder . . .

THE SUBSTANCE OF A SHADE

John Glasby

Soon after moving into Mexton Grange, an old Georgian country house in the Cotswolds, Alice hears disquieting stories and rumours about her new abode: the previous owners had been driven out by a strange, oppressive atmosphere in the house. It was not as if the house was *actually* haunted — rather, it was as if the house was *waiting to be haunted* . . . These five stories of terror and the macabre by John Glasby will tingle the spine on any dark and stormy night.

THE GLASS HOUSE

V. J. Banis

When Antoinette swindled Margaree out of the old estate on Cape Breton Island, Margaree swore on her mother's grave that she'd win it back. But blocking her ambition are three deadly obstacles: the formidable Antoinette; her treacherous son; and Jean, whom she loves deeply but who hates the old house with all his heart. To win Jean, Margaree would have to give up the estate. The key to it all lies somewhere within the mysterious reaches of the Glass House . . . if Margaree remains alive long enough to find it!